"Are you always this grumpy?" Miriam asked mildly.

"Ja."

She shrugged. "I feel responsible," she replied. "If I hadn't hit you with my car, you wouldn't have a broken arm. But what's done is done. I'll leave you for now and be back early tomorrow."

Without another word, she slid back into the driver's seat and drove away.

Major greeted him with overwhelming enthusiasm. The dog never stared, never judged him about his appearance. He merely accepted him.

Now that he thought about it, so did Miriam. She was one of the few people he'd met in the last three years who didn't negatively react to his ravaged face.

He ran a hand through his hair and made his way to the house. A bowl of eggs rested on the table. Major's bowl was full of food.

How did she know what to do? Aaron was grudgingly impressed.

It seemed he had a helper…whether he wanted it or not.

And she was beautiful.

Living on a remote self-sufficient homestead in North Idaho, **Patrice Lewis** is a Christian wife, mother, author, blogger, columnist and speaker. She has practiced and written about rural subjects for almost thirty years. When she isn't writing, Patrice enjoys self-sufficiency projects, such as animal husbandry, small-scale dairy production, gardening, food preservation and canning, and homeschooling. She and her husband have been married since 1990 and have two daughters.

Books by Patrice Lewis

Love Inspired

The Amish Newcomer
Amish Baby Lessons
Her Path to Redemption
The Amish Animal Doctor
The Mysterious Amish Nanny
Their Road to Redemption
The Amish Midwife's Bargain

Visit the Author Profile page at LoveInspired.com.

The Amish Midwife's Bargain

Patrice Lewis

Recycling programs for this product may not exist in your area.

ISBN-13: 978-1-335-59702-1

The Amish Midwife's Bargain

For questions and comments about the quality of this book, please contact us at CustomerService@Harlequin.com.

Love Inspired
22 Adelaide St. West, 41st Floor
Toronto, Ontario M5H 4E3, Canada
www.LoveInspired.com

Printed in U.S.A.

He healeth the broken in heart,
and bindeth up their wounds.
—*Psalm* 147:3

To my husband and daughters,
my greatest earthly joy.
To Jesus, for His redeeming grace.
To God, who has blessed me more than
I could possibly deserve.

Chapter One

It was a dark and stormy night. Those clichéd words ran through Miriam Kemp's mind as she peered through the darkened, rain-washed windshield of her car. She was tired after a long day's drive and anxious to reach her brother's home.

The storm had rolled in fifteen minutes before, rising over the Bitterroot Mountains to the west and sending ominous flashes of lightning across the valley below. Following her brother's directions, Miriam passed through the tiny and isolated town of Pierce, Montana—population 3,500—and turned onto a gravel road toward the Amish settlement that lay three miles beyond.

What she hadn't anticipated was the major thunderstorm that had made the early May landscape impossible to see.

Her brother, Thomas, had written of the area's natural beauty—its massive range of mountains, the flat and fertile valley at its base, the coniferous trees that all but hid the town—and assured her it was nothing like the settled and crowded places in Indiana, where she had come from.

Squinting through the flapping windshield wipers, Miriam slowed her speed still further, searching for an address number for her brother's house. This part of the valley had very few buildings, and farms seemed to be widely scattered and far apart. It was almost as dark as night, and it would be all she needed to—

A huge black canine shape flung itself across the road, illuminated by a flash of lightning. Miriam gasped. The dog had come perilously close to her wheels, and she was glad she wasn't going any faster.

Distracted by the dog, Miriam glanced to her right. An instant later, her eyes back on the road, she screamed and slammed on her brakes as a man's figure appeared in front of her.

It was too late. With a shout, the man threw up his arms and disappeared from view.

Adrenaline flooded her system, but instinct took over. Snatching her cell phone from the seat next to her, she yanked open the car door and dashed outside into the pouring rain.

By the car's headlights, she saw the man unconscious on the ground, his arm bent in an unnatural position, the rain pounding over him.

And there was more. The left side of his face was a mass of twisted flesh and heavy scarring. For one gut-wrenching moment, she thought the impact of her car had caused the disfigurement, until she realized the scars were old.

She dropped to her knees and began a survey of his vitals. Airway and respiration clear, pulse strong, bleeding moderate, arm probably broken. She snatched up her cell phone and dialed for help.

"911, what is your emergency?" came a calm female voice.

"I just hit a man who ran right in front of my car," barked Miriam. She described her location and the man's condition, then added, "I have EMT training and will keep him stable until help arrives."

"Dispatching immediately," replied the operator.

Miriam scrabbled to her feet and rummaged the hatchback car until she found a coat, which she used to cover the man's face and upper body from the relentless rain. Her own clothes were soaking wet, but she hardly noticed. Instead, she began searching through the packed possessions in the car, knowing she had an emergency bag and furious with herself that she had stacked boxes and suitcases on top of it.

Unable to locate the bag without completely unloading the vehicle, she returned to the unconscious man and continued to monitor his vitals, holding the coat aloft to keep the rain off his face. There was blood on his face stemming from a cut on his scalp, but it didn't seem serious. It matted his dark brown hair and emphasized the deep scarring. Looking more closely, Miriam recognized the scars as healed burn marks.

The man groaned and attempted to move, and Miriam tried to hold him still while holding the coat over his face with the other. She wasn't sure how conscious he was, but she said, "An ambulance is on the way. Best not to move."

The heart of the thunderstorm had passed by the time

she saw the welcome flashing lights of an approaching ambulance. The rain began to relent as well.

Within moments, the emergency vehicle pulled to a stop, and a crew of first responders emerged and swarmed around the man. Miriam stepped away to let them work.

While they slipped a foam collar around his neck and transferred him to a gurney, Miriam saw a police car with two officers inside pull up behind. Miriam went over to speak with them as they exited the vehicle.

"He ran right in front of me," she explained, trying to keep her voice professional but hearing it tremble. Delayed adrenaline had hit her system. "A dog dashed across the road moments before, so I'm guessing he was chasing the animal. It all happened at the height of the storm, so visual conditions were bad. I'm guessing I was going ten miles per hour at the moment I hit him."

"Can you accompany us to the hospital?" one officer asked, wiping rain off his glasses. "We can do a full write-up while the patient is assessed."

"Yes, of course. Is there a hospital in town?"

"Yes." The officer eyed her. "You must not be from around here."

"No. I'm from Indiana. I was traveling to visit my brother and his wife, who live nearby." She pointed to the license plate of her vehicle.

"Not a good start to your visit," quipped the other officer.

"Not at all," she agreed. She hugged herself, chilled in her wet clothing. She swallowed back tears at the thought of hurting another human. "I just pray the man will be okay."

The door to the back of the ambulance slammed shut.

The police officers instructed Miriam to turn her vehicle around and follow it, and they would follow her.

Ten minutes later, she parked near the emergency entrance to the town's small hospital. Miriam grabbed her purse and exited the car. The rain had eased to a light shower.

For the next hour, Miriam answered the police's questions, and provided documentation and explained the circumstances of the accident. And prayed the man would be okay. She felt dreadfully responsible.

"You're free to go, ma'am," one of the officers finally said. "We'll be in touch at the phone number you gave us, and at your brother's address."

"I wonder if I could see the man?" she asked. "I'm a registered nurse. I'm used to helping people heal, not putting them in the hospital."

"That's up to the hospital personnel."

Left alone in the waiting room, Miriam approached the front desk and inquired about the man's status.

"I believe he's having his arm set right now," the receptionist explained. "He's regained consciousness, but we'll keep him overnight to monitor him."

"I'm a registered nurse in Indiana," explained Miriam. "I know this is an unorthodox request, but I would like permission to stay and monitor him. I feel so terribly guilty."

The receptionist looked startled. "That's not normally done, and we're outside of visiting hours. But if you take a seat in the waiting room, I'll ask the doctor on call to speak with you."

Miriam nodded and went to take a seat. Usually, she

was on the other side of those double doors, not in the waiting room.

She was determined to see the man. She felt a heavy burden of responsibility for his fate.

But what could she do? She tried bargaining with *Gott*, willing to do something—anything—to show her remorse for the accident. Hopefully *Gott* would show her the answer.

When Aaron Lapp woke up, he was in a dark room, lying on a bed. He tried to lift his left arm, then realized it was encased in a heavy cast.

Another hospital. He hated hospitals. He felt shame and almost panic that he was among the *Englisch*. In his experience, the *Englisch* did not react well when they saw his face.

"Don't try to move," he heard a woman say.

He looked over and saw a young woman in *Englisch* garb—a muddy blouse and mud-spattered skirt—rise from a chair and approach the bed.

His mind felt thick. "Hospital?" he croaked.

"Yes. They let me stay so I could keep watch over you."

"Who are you?"

"I accidentally hit you with my car."

"Don't remember..." he mumbled, then drifted off.

When he woke up again, the room was filled with dim pre-dawn light, and the same woman was still there, slumped in a chair, fast asleep.

Aaron's mind felt a bit clearer, and he tried to puzzle out what had happened. Something to do with his dog, Major, and then...?

And then he'd woken up in a hospital room. He didn't remember anything more.

But he didn't want to be here. He didn't want to be anywhere except his farm and among the church members, where his disfigured face no longer caused comment. But here among the *Englisch*, he knew he could expect everything from mute curiosity to gasps of shock.

He glanced down at the cast on his arm and felt a moment of anxiety. He had livestock to maintain, cows to milk, chickens to feed. He didn't have time to lie here in a hospital bed. How was he supposed to milk his cows with a broken arm?

He tried to move and realized how battered and bruised he felt. Without meaning to, he groaned from the pain.

The woman woke up instantly. She blinked the sleep from her eyes, then sprang to her feet. "You're awake."

He automatically searched for the obligatory reaction on her face and saw nothing. Instead, as he tried to sit up, she aided him with surprising dexterity—moving the mechanized bed into an upright position and propping a pillow behind his back.

"I imagine you're sore," she said. "Hang on, I'm going to call the nurse for some pain medication."

She disappeared from his sight before he could stop her. He didn't want to see a nurse. He didn't want to see anyone—though he supposed it could hardly be helped in a hospital.

Who was she? Why was she in his hospital room? He vaguely remembered talking to her, but his mind was clouded, and he couldn't remember anything else.

In a few moments, the woman returned, followed by an older nurse dressed in scrubs.

"Good morning!" the nurse said brightly. Too brightly. He was familiar with the pathetic attempts by strangers to ignore his scars. "How do you feel this morning?"

"Confused," Aaron mumbled. "What happened?"

The young woman hesitated. "I hit you with my car last night. I wanted to stay and make sure you were all right."

Aaron's mind buzzed, but he felt too foggy to form intelligent questions. Instead, he watched as the nurse tipped two pills out of a bottle and handed them to him, along with a glass of water.

"Pain medicine," she clarified.

He nodded and swallowed the pills, choking them down with water. Then he rested his head back on the pillow.

"I can't stay here," he informed the nurse. "I have livestock to take care of."

"Who are you?" asked the younger woman. "You didn't have any identification on you when they brought you in last night."

"My name is Aaron Lapp," he replied. "I live out in the settlement."

"The Amish settlement?"

"Ja."

"Do you know my brother Thomas Kemp?"

"Your brother?"

"Yes, my name is Miriam Kemp. Thomas is my brother."

"Thomas Kemp is my closest neighbor."

"I see." Miriam looked at the nurse. "This will make it easy, then."

"Make what easy?" Aaron felt irritable.

"Taking care of you. Since I'm staying at my brother's, I can walk over every day and cook your meals."

"How about milking my cows?" he said sarcastically. He gestured toward the cast on his arm. "It's hard to maintain a dairy farm one-handed."

She smiled. "Okay."

"'Okay' what?"

"'Okay,' I'll milk your cows."

"What would you know about cows?"

"Mr. Lapp, I started milking cows when I was ten years old."

He was silenced. It hardly seemed likely that an *Englisch* woman would know how to milk cows—but then again, if she was Thomas Kemp's sister, that must mean she had been raised Amish…

His head swam. The pain medication had not yet taken effect, and he felt like his whole body was one large bruise.

"Fine," he grunted. "It's the least you can do after hitting me with your car."

"Now, now," soothed the nurse. "She's just trying to help."

"I wouldn't need help if she hadn't hit me."

He saw her stiffen. "You're right," she snapped. "That's why I'm offering my services."

"Fine." He just wanted her to go away.

As if reading his thoughts, she stood up. "Then I'll be going. I haven't seen my brother yet, so I have a lot to tell him." She nodded, thanked the nurse and walked out of the room.

He looked at the nurse. "What was all that about?" he asked in bewilderment.

The older woman chuckled. "It looks like you're going to have a caretaker—both for you and your animals."

"But she's a stranger."

"Well, it sounds like she'll be a neighbor."

"Great," he grunted. His arm throbbed, and his head hurt. "How much longer do I have to stay here?"

"The doctor wants to keep you until tomorrow."

"Then I sure hope she *can* milk cows," he muttered.

"So you have a dairy farm?" The nurse seemed inclined to be chatty.

But Aaron didn't like to *chat*. He far preferred silence. Silence and solitude. "*Ja*," he said shortly. "And cows need to be milked."

"You're welcome to call your neighbor to make arrangements."

"We're Amish. We don't have phones," he reminded her.

At her startled expression, Aaron felt ashamed. "I'm sorry," he said. "I'm not used to being around people much."

The older woman elevated her eyebrows. "I see. Well, Mr. Lapp, I suggest you get some rest. You're going to be in a bit of pain until those pills take effect. I need to check on my other patients. Excuse me."

Aaron felt like kicking himself. He had managed to irritate first Miriam Kemp, then the nurse. What a monster he was.

He let out an irritable sigh. He *was* a monster. A

long time ago, Aaron had read a book about a man who haunted an opera house, ashamed to be seen because his face was deformed and living his life vicariously through music. He and the character in that book had a lot in common.

There was another story he remembered from when he was a child, this one involving a beautiful young woman imprisoned by a beast. In the end, however, the beast became a handsome prince.

Those kinds of things didn't happen in real life.

Instead, Aaron had to face the reality that he would be a beast forever. The woman he had courted back in Pennsylvania had told him as much, that she couldn't marry anyone like him after the accident.

So Aaron had turned his back on Pennsylvania and the people he'd grown up with and moved to Montana. Facing a life alone, he'd voluntarily imprisoned himself in a cell of his own making. He couldn't wait to get out of this hospital and back to his farm, where his animals never stood in judgment of him.

He loved his farm, his livestock, his dog and cats. The animals were his family now, and he missed them terribly.

Gradually, his eyes closed, and he welcomed the momentary extinguishing of the pain, both physical and emotional.

Just before he drifted off, an unwelcome thought flittered through his brain. What was he going to do with a woman hanging around his farm?

Chapter Two

Now that the weather had cleared and the sun had dawned, it was much easier for Miriam to find her way to her brother Thomas's home. She also had a chance to admire the scenery.

This corner of Montana was beautiful. Thomas had said the area became browner as the summer progressed, but this early in the season, everything was lush and green. The high mountains to the west still had snow. As she found her way to the Amish settlement, she saw an abundance of verdant fields. Conifers were the dominant tree in the area.

Retracing her path from last night, she traveled the gravel road, passing newly established farms and waving to an occasional buggy, the occupants peering at her with astonishment. Evidently, motorized vehicles weren't common in the settlement.

If she planned to stay here, she would have to sell her car and phone. She wouldn't need these modern conveniences anymore. Instead, she would once again adopt the culture of her youth and return to the church in which she had been raised.

Gone would be the long hours working in hospitals. Gone would be the life-and-death responsibility that every medical professional faced. That was behind her now. She had tried her best, but because of her, a young mother and her unborn baby had died. She had prayed to *Gott* for forgiveness and pledged Him her vocation in return.

Following the slip of paper with directions, she pulled up before a small cottage. It was a pretty little place, with Virginia creeper twining around porch rails and a huge garden in front, newly planted and fenced tightly against deer.

She switched off the ignition and emerged from the car, stretching out her back. Sleeping in a chair at the hospital last night hadn't done her any favors.

The door flung open, and Thomas walked out, his face lit up. "Miriam!"

"Thomas!" She dashed for the house.

Her brother met her at the bottom of the porch steps and enveloped her in a huge bear hug. "It's so *gut* to see you!"

She blinked back tears. Her baby brother had, by the grace of *Gott*, straightened himself out. After living a life of petty crime back in Indiana, he'd turned over a new leaf, moved to Montana, gotten baptized and married. He was so different than the troubled young man she remembered that she almost didn't recognize him. His face wore an expression of peace beneath the excitement of their reunion.

"How was your trip?" he asked, turning to mount the porch steps.

Before she could respond, a woman and child stepped onto the porch. The woman had dark—almost black—hair and chocolate brown eyes, wore a welcoming smile, and sported a huge belly under her loose-fitting dress. *Seven months along*, thought Miriam.

"Miriam, this is my wife, Emma," said Thomas proudly.

"How do you do?" Miriam held out a hand, but with a cluck, Emma bypassed the hand and smothered her in a hug as well. "We're so glad you're here safely. Thomas has talked of nothing else for days."

Miriam felt the warmth of her sister-in-law's embrace and knew her brother had chosen his spouse wisely.

"And who is this?" Miriam inquired, dropping to one knee to smile at the little girl.

"This is my daughter, Hannah," replied Emma. "Hannah, say hello to your *tante* Miriam."

"H'lo," the child said, giving Miriam a lovely smile.

"Come inside, come inside," said Thomas. "We were just about to have breakfast. Are you hungry?"

"*Ja*, actually, I am."

The house was the scene of contented domestic chaos, with children's toys and books scattered around and an unlit wood cookstove located between the kitchen and living room areas. "I've got biscuits in the oven," said Emma, peering inside a propane stove. "They're not quite done yet."

"Anything I can do?" inquired Miriam.

"You can pour yourself a cup of *kaffi*—or tea, if you prefer—and tell us about your trip." Emma gestured toward the kitchen counter, where coffee and tea were laid out.

"*Ja*," agreed Thomas, pouring himself a cup of coffee and seating himself at the kitchen table. "We expected you last night. What happened?"

"I accidentally hit your neighbor Aaron Lapp with my car," replied Miriam.

Her brother and Emma jerked upright, staring. "W-what?" croaked Thomas.

"You heard me." Emma poured herself some tea and sat at the table. "During that huge thunderstorm last night, I was creeping along, and a huge dog suddenly darted right in front of me on the road, and I guess Aaron was chasing him. I didn't see him until too late. Ran into him and broke his arm. I called an ambulance and stabilized him until it arrived, then went with him to the hospital, where I watched over him overnight."

Emma dropped onto a kitchen chair. "I-is he *oll recht*?"

"He's fine, if a little grumpy."

Thomas waved a hand. "He's always grumpy—don't take it personally. What a start to your visit, Miriam."

"I know, right?" She gave a wan smile. "Not my best moment. However, I told Aaron I'd look after him while he recovers, including milking his cows. Will you show me where he lives after breakfast?"

Thomas smiled. "He's almost directly across the road from us. You can see his driveway from here, though his house is set back a bit behind some trees."

"I was praying *Gott* would show me how to make it up to the man, when He gave me the answer," Miriam remarked. "Because of my actions, Aaron can't work his farm until his arm is healed, so I'll do what I can to work it for him."

"It's not that big a farm," said Emma. "He only has six milk cows. I assume you know how to milk?"

"*Ja*, it's one of the chores I always enjoyed. But I don't know his milking schedule, so that's why I should probably go milk them right after breakfast. I don't want the ladies to get too uncomfortable."

"I believe he only milks once a day," said Emma, standing to check the biscuits. She snatched up a pair of hot pads and pulled two trays from the oven. "He leaves the calves with their mothers and only separates them at night, then milks in the morning. He says he gets plenty of milk to sell or use for cheese that way, and it doesn't overwhelm him." Emma transferred the biscuits to a plate and brought them, along with jam and butter, to the table.

Along with the others, Miriam said a blessing over the food, then reached for a biscuit. "Tell me about Aaron," she said. "What happened to his face?"

"Burned," replied Thomas, talking in between bites of biscuit. "He's never explained the circumstances. He moved out here from Pennsylvania a couple years ago. He barely leaves his farm except for church. He's a fair carpenter and will join the men for building projects, but doesn't say much and rarely smiles."

"Sad," murmured Miriam. "The burn unit was always one of the most traumatic to work in."

"Thomas said you're leaving nursing behind?" inquired Emma.

"Ja." Miriam scrubbed a hand over her face as if to wipe away memories. "I was starting to specialize in

midwifery. I loved it—until I lost a patient. I—I promised *Gott* I would give up medicine if He could forgive me."

"*Gott* works in mysterious ways," Thomas remarked. "Don't be surprised if that promise is challenged."

Miriam didn't feel like discussing the depths of her despair and guilt over the incident. Nor did she focus on the emptiness inside her from what used to be a satisfying career. What would she do now? She didn't know.

She was glad to work Aaron's farm in the meantime. It gave her hope and a sense of purpose for the immediate future.

Aaron moved around the hospital room restlessly, dressed in his dry-but-muddy clothes, wishing he could leave. He'd had his fill of hospitals after the accident three years ago. Now he felt like a prisoner.

His broken arm ached, but it was manageable. His body was sore, but it was nothing he couldn't handle. He just wanted out. Now.

At last, the doctor stopped by. "I gather you're anxious to leave, Mr. Lapp," he said dryly, regarding Aaron with an amused expression.

"I have livestock to attend. I can't stay here," he said curtly.

"I'd say you're ready to go," the doctor replied. "And since you have a ride, I'm willing to sign off on your release."

"I have a ride?" Aaron repeated in surprise.

"Yes, someone is driving you home."

"Who?"

"I don't know. She's waiting for you downstairs in the lobby."

"She?" Could it be Miriam Kemp? He knew no one else in the community with a car.

"Yes, *she*. We'll expect you back in about seven weeks, Mr. Lapp, so we can remove your cast."

"*Ja*, that's fine. Can I go now?"

"Yes, you can go now."

"Thank you." Without another word, Aaron walked out of the hospital room.

Sure enough, there in the lobby, Miriam sat, glancing through a magazine. To his shock, she was dressed entirely as an Amish woman—dark green dress, apron, white *kapp*. She rose to her feet as he walked through the double doors.

"Ready to go?" she said cheerfully.

"How did you know when I was going to be released today?"

"I asked."

Aaron felt his cheeks heat. "Oh."

Outside the hospital, he blinked in the summer sunshine and wished for his hat. Miriam led the way toward a dark blue hatchback vehicle.

"Hop in," she invited him, opening the passenger-side door.

Without a word, he slid inside and stared ahead. Miriam seated herself behind the steering wheel, fastened her seat belt and started the vehicle.

Miriam eased the car into traffic, and within minutes she was heading out of town, toward the Amish settlement, where the road turned to gravel.

The silence in the car continued. Aaron was faintly

surprised. Women tended to chatter, but Miriam remained quiet. She didn't seem happy or sad or intimidated or angry. She was just…quiet.

At last, she turned up the drive to his pretty but smallish log cabin with a generous front porch and a single rocking chair. Inside the fenced yard, his enormous black Newfoundland, Major, pranced around, wagging his tail.

Aaron fumbled with the door handle and stood up outside the vehicle. She also got out and looked at him over the hood.

"I hope you don't mind that I trespassed in your house and barn," she informed him. "You'll find all six of your cows have been milked. I also fed them and released them into the pasture. I fed and watered the horses and the chickens, and gathered the eggs. Your dog and cats have been fed too."

He stood there, perplexed. "*Danke*," he finally sputtered.

She gave him a thin smile. "I'll be back early tomorrow. I wouldn't mind a proper tour of the place, if I'm going to be doing the work until your arm heals."

"Why are you doing this?" he retorted,

"Are you always this grumpy?" she asked mildly.

"Ja."

She shrugged. "I feel responsible," she replied. "If I hadn't hit you with my car, you wouldn't have a broken arm. But what's done is done. I'll leave you for now and be back early tomorrow."

Without another word, she slid back into the driver's seat, started the engine and drove away.

Aaron stared after her until the car disappeared from sight. Then he turned and made his way to the yard's gate.

Major greeted him with overwhelming enthusiasm, and Aaron smiled at the dog as he never did to people. The dog never stared, never judged him for his appearance. He merely accepted him.

Now that he thought about it, so did Miriam. She was one of the few people he'd met in the last three years who hadn't reacted negatively to his ravaged face.

Curious, he skirted the house and went toward the barn. Sure enough, his six Jersey cows and their young calves were peacefully chewing their cud in the pasture. A fast tour of the barn revealed that it had been cleaned up, and fresh hay had been added to the feed boxes. The barn cats prowled around his legs, and he saw their feeder was full. The chickens clucked in their spacious enclosure.

He ran a hand through his hair and made his way to the house. Inside the icebox was the morning's milk, neatly strained and covered with the cloth caps he used. A bowl of eggs rested on the table. Major's dish was full of food.

How had she known what to do? Aaron was grudgingly impressed. It seemed he had a helper—whether he wanted one or not—until his arm was healed.

And there was no question he couldn't handle the chores himself. It was impossible to milk cows one-handed.

He wondered if he could tolerate another person on the farm all day. He was used to his solitude and wasn't sure he liked the idea of Miriam's constant presence. On the other hand, he recognized he had no option.

But wow, was she pretty. Aaron remembered the ache in his heart when his fiancée had dumped him. He'd avoided women ever since. How was it that Miriam could overlook his scarred face?

Chapter Three

That afternoon, Miriam sat with her sister-in-law in her cozy kitchen, becoming better acquainted. Talk soon turned to Aaron. "Thomas mentioned he's always grumpy, and Aaron himself admitted it." Miriam chuckled. "But I suspect a lot of it is because he's in pain and just doesn't want to admit it."

"Hmm, maybe some of it." Emma stirred a pot on the stove. "But I know it's because he's ashamed of how he looks. He's often snappish. Just try not to take any of it personally."

"I won't, I promise." Miriam picked up some work gloves and the rubber boots Emma had loaned her so she could stay clean while mucking out the barn. "Meanwhile, I intend to have him give me some guidance on what to do on his farm, so I don't know when I'll be back."

"Bye, *Tante* Miriam," said little Hannah.

"Bye-bye, sweetie." Miriam dropped a kiss on the child's head and stepped outside.

The May air was cool this early in the morning. It

took only ten minutes to walk to Aaron's place. She didn't know what time he normally got up, so she bypassed the house and went straight for the barn.

Except she needed the buckets she'd sterilized yesterday, which were still in his kitchen. Miriam stood, undecided, for a moment, then headed for the house. Quietly, she opened the back door and tiptoed into the kitchen.

A dark shape startled her, until she recognized it was Major, the enormous Newfoundland. "Good morning, you troublemaker," she told him, scratching the dog on the head. The huge animal pressed against her leg, looking for more affection, until he nearly pushed her over and she had to grab the countertop to steady herself.

"He seems to like you," Aaron said from behind.

Miriam gasped and whirled around, pressing a hand to her chest. "Gracious, you startled me!"

"That's what you get for sneaking into the house at dawn."

"I needed the milk buckets. I hope I didn't wake you." His shirt was untucked and he was barefoot. He looked rumpled and cross, and his scarred face appeared craggy in the early morning light. "How do you feel?"

"Sore," he admitted.

"Have you taken your pain medication today?"

"Not yet. I just got up."

"Don't put it off. You'll find you'll feel so much better once it kicks in."

"What are you, a nurse?" he snapped.

"As a matter of fact, *ja*."

His jaw dropped open. "You're kidding."

"No. I'm an EMT and registered nurse, also certified in midwifery. At least, I was back in Indiana." She couldn't help but smile at the shocked look on his face.

"Then what are you doing milking my cows?"

"Just that. Milking your cows and otherwise keeping your farm running until you're recovered." She sighed. "Don't argue with me, Aaron. I just arrived yesterday to visit my brother and stay here in Montana for a while. I don't have a job at the moment and would be bored out of my gourd if I don't do something productive."

"Okay, but..."

"So I suggest you get properly dressed, take your pain pills, and then come show me around and tell me what needs to be done each day."

He looked a bit dazed. Without a word, he turned around and she heard a door close. She almost chuckled. Sometimes nurses had to be bossy.

She seized the buckets she had washed yesterday and made her way to the barn. She wasn't sure in what order Aaron milked his cows, but by watching them for a few moments, she selected the one that seemed most dominant. She clipped a lead rope to the animal's halter and brought her into the milking stall. Then she sat on a crate, put one of the buckets beneath the udder and started milking.

The sound zinging into the metal pail and the fresh sweet smell brought back memories from her childhood, when her father had first taught her. She'd always loved milking cows. It was no hardship to rediscover the skill.

The barn cats snaked around her feet and the cow's legs, meowing. Miriam paused to pour some warm milk in a shallow bowl, and the four cats settled down to lap up the treat.

A noise made her look up. Aaron walked into the barn, looking much more pulled together, though his shirt was badly tucked, no doubt due to the cast on his arm.

"You seem to know what you're doing," he admitted, standing next to the cow.

"*Ja*. It's like riding a bicycle. It's hard to forget. Your cows are very sweet too. You must treat them very well."

She was surprised to see a gentler look come over his face as he patted the animal she was milking. "*Ja*, I love my cows," he said. "I love all my animals. They… they don't judge." He turned away.

So that was it. Pain—the emotional kind—was clear from Aaron's posture as he stood stiffly looking out at the pasture.

"What do you do with all this milk?" she inquired.

"I make cheese and butter, and sell it at an Amish-run store in town. I also have a fair number of people in our church who buy fresh milk from me."

"I see."

After a moment of silence between them, he blurted out, "You're a nurse?"

"*Ja.*"

"But you're Amish."

"I used to be. I hope to be again." She didn't feel like getting into her background. "Hand me that other bucket, will you?"

It took forty minutes to finish hand-milking the six cows, and Miriam's hands were tired by the end of it. She was out of practice, she realized.

Throughout the process, Aaron stood by but said little, though he helpfully led the finished cows out of the barn to reunite them with their hungry calves.

"I process the milk in the house," he clarified as he seized one of the buckets. Miriam followed with two more. "By the way, I have a milk canister. I fill it as I milk, then strap it to a hand truck. It makes it easier to transport all the milk to the house at once."

"*Gut* to know." She trailed behind him to the cabin.

Now that she had a chance to view it more closely, the inside of the cabin needed a bit of help. It was definitely a bachelor's home, full of dusty furnishings, dingy windows and unswept floors. Surprisingly, he had a wall of books in the living room—an unbroken sweep of bookshelves at least twelve-feet wide and six-feet high and completely packed with volumes. It was an impressive collection for such a small house, and she wondered how often the books served as a substitute for company. She understood. She had way too many books herself.

However unkempt the rest of the house, though, she soon learned his milk-processing methods were conducted under the strictest sanitation. And very nearly the strictest silence.

After the milk had been strained and the buckets sterilized, she finally remarked, "You don't talk much, do you?"

He shrugged. "I don't have anything to say."

"Actually, I'll bet you have plenty of interesting things to say," she retorted. "You're just choosing not to say them."

He eyed her, looking grim through his scarred face. "If I do or if I don't, that's my business."

"Well, it's my business as long as I'm working here." She covered the last of the strained milk with a clean weighted cloth and, per his instructions, put the jars in a dedicated icebox. She turned and made a show of dusting off her hands. "Now, I'm requesting a complete tour of your farm, both inside and outside. It's hard to fill in for you when I have to guess or search where things are."

His mouth pursed as if he had swallowed a lemon, but he capitulated. "All right, then, let's start in here."

He walked her around the cabin. Privately, she thought it was far more geared toward practicality than comfort. It was very much a man's solitary space, with a single comfortable reclining chair inside, a single kitchen chair at the table and a single rocking chair on the porch. Did he never have guests? It was a sobering thought.

The kitchen was the only truly clean place in the house. "I have to keep everything as sterile as possible," he explained, showing her the pots and strainers he used to make cheese, the butter churn, and molds. He shrugged away the state of the rest of the cabin. "I live alone. I don't care what it looks like."

But Miriam did. Her brothers had always accused her of having too tender a heart, but she found Aaron's place achingly sad. The little cabin had the potential to be cozy and welcoming, but instead there was an air of neglect, or rather, indifference. It spoke strongly about Aaron's frame of mind. She wondered just how deep those scars ran.

"Now, show me how you like your livestock chores done," she said. "You can walk me through a typical morning. Unless you're too tired? I don't want to wear you out."

"I'm fine," he snapped. "Just helpless, thanks to you." He waved his cast.

Miriam, all too familiar with how pain altered peoples' personalities, set her mind toward patience and understanding of his shortness and ill temper. She tightened her jaw, smiled and followed him out the door.

"What's your dog's name?" she inquired as the massive canine loped toward them, tongue lolling.

"Major."

"And why were you chasing him through the thunderstorm?"

He stared at her blankly. "Was I chasing him?"

"Ah, you don't remember." She nodded. "A typical response to trauma. Yes, I was driving through the storm, looking for my brother's address, when Major dashed right in front of my car. I didn't see you until it was too late." She shuddered at the memory. "I feel terrible about hitting you."

"And so you should."

Miriam clenched her teeth.

The moment the unkind words were out of his mouth, Aaron wanted to snatch them back. Miriam was doing her best to make up for the accident. He would be a fool to chase her away, especially since he had no other way to take care of his animals while his arm was healing.

But his social skills had atrophied in the last three years. He hardly knew how to be civil, especially to a woman. He was too used to seeing shuttered expressions and skittering avoidance.

But Miriam not only *didn't* avoid him—she waded

in with both feet encased in rubber boots, ready to do battle on his behalf and take care of his farm.

It was strange to have another person around, much less a woman who seemed frighteningly competent.

So he showed her around.

"How many acres do you have?" she asked.

"Fifty. I have about twenty acres in hay, fifteen in grazing and the rest as a woodlot."

"Nice breakdown," she commented. "It means you have the potential to be fairly self-sufficient."

He glanced at her sharply. "*Completely* self-sufficient," he corrected. He was astounded she had assessed his objective with such accuracy. "That's my goal."

"Why?"

"So I never have to leave home."

"I see." She looked thoughtfully around the barn, with its calf pens, milking stall, feed boxes, hay storage and horse stalls. "This represents a lot of work. I'm surprised you managed it alone."

"It's what I prefer. It's my full-time job."

"Hmm. What about things normally done by women? Gardening, canning, that kind of thing?"

"I do that too."

She raised her eyebrows. "This must keep you busy."

"*Ja*, all the time. It's better than the alternative." He turned on his heel. His chatter was too close to the truth, so he changed the subject. "You've already seen the chicken coop, I assume?"

"Just long enough to make sure the birds had food."

"I don't feed them grain, except sometimes in winter. This time of year, they live off the compost pile as well as fresh forage." He didn't feel like explaining the particulars of permaculture or alternative feeds. He just didn't want her wasting grain when it wasn't necessary.

"So what chores do you want me to do each morning and afternoon?"

He turned his back and gazed out at the pasture. "Pretty much what you've already done. Milking, cleaning stalls, feeding. I may walk you through making cheese since I need to process the milk almost daily just to keep up. Think you can handle everything?" he asked in a challenging tone.

She shrugged. "Let's just say this will be my full-time job for the time being."

Grudgingly, he was impressed. She seemed impervious to his admittedly bad temper. Thomas Kemp's sister was unlike any other woman he'd met.

"Well, then." His arm throbbed, and he was far wearier than he wanted to admit. "I'm going to lie down for a while. I'll leave you to it."

"That's fine. I'll stay busy."

He nodded, turned his back to her and strode up to the house with faithful Major at his side.

Once inside, he swallowed the pain pills he had avoided earlier in hopes he could tough things out. He couldn't. His arm hurt a lot, his head pounded, his body ached and he wanted nothing more than to sleep for a couple of hours.

He made his way into the bedroom, stretched out fully clothed and fell into a deep sleep.

When he blinked himself awake, a glance at the bedside clock confirmed he'd slept for several hours. He grunted in surprise. It wasn't like him to nap—normally, he worked from dawn until dusk—but considering his injury, he supposed it was not surprising. Then his stomach growled. He'd forgotten to eat all day.

He stumbled up from the bed, splashed his face in the bathroom, and emerged to a complete and utter surprise.

Miriam had taken over the kitchen. She was cooking something that smelled mouth-wateringly delicious. With her back to him, she hadn't noticed him, so he took the opportunity to examine her.

She was slim and a bit on the tall side. Her honey-colored hair curled a bit at the nape of her neck, not quite covered by her *kapp*. And she was humming.

The homey simplicity of the scene was something he'd missed in the last three years. He couldn't remember the last time a woman had been in his house. He'd hoped his fiancée, Denise, would take over his kitchen, but after the fire…

Miriam turned and jerked a bit in surprise. "Gracious, you startled me! I'm glad to see you up. How do you feel?"

Feel? How could he ever confess to her how he truly felt? It was a far more loaded question than she must have anticipated.

"*Oll recht*," he answered blandly, then added, "I didn't expect to sleep for so long."

"I'm sure you needed it." She turned to stir something on the stove.

"Whatever you're making smells wonderful."

"Just a beef stew and some fresh bread. I hope you don't mind that I rummaged through your pantry. You have an admirable amount of things canned up, so it wasn't hard to pull together a meal. Did you really do all the canning by yourself?"

"*Ja*. I'm a *gut* canner now." He glanced into the living room and blinked in surprise. It was spotless, shining with a subdued glow in the early-afternoon sun, the likes of which he'd never seen. Even the books looked like they'd been dusted.

"W-what did you do in the living room?" he stuttered.

"Just cleaned it up." She chuckled. "You're something of a slob, Aaron Lapp, if I do say so. But it was nothing a little dusting and mopping couldn't cure. Here, see if this stew is any good." She scooped out some stew into a bowl, slathered some fresh butter on a warm slice of bread and put everything on the table.

It was all Aaron could do to remember to say a blessing to *Gott* before diving in. The food was amazing. "Oh my," he mumbled, finally coming up for air.

"You like it?"

"*Ja*. It's…it's incredible." He rose to fill his bowl a second time.

Miriam chuckled. "I'm glad."

"You don't have to cook for me, you know. As long as my animals are cared for, that's all I need."

"Really?" She turned a surprised face to him. "You don't need hot food and a clean house? I thought those things were universal."

He hardened his heart against the stark longing. He didn't need anyone's pity. But for once, he tempered his harsh thoughts with some diplomacy.

"You're not here to be my maid," he clarified. "I can get by, except for stuff like milking the cows."

"I'm amazed at everything you do," she responded.

"But why are you resisting something I'm voluntarily offering? Right now I'm between jobs. I have nothing else to do. I don't mind working here."

"Why is that?" He bit into a slice of fresh bread and spoke with his mouth full. "I know you said you're here to visit your brother, but how long is the visit? Didn't you have plans for while you're here?"

It was as if a shutter dropped over her face, wiping away all expression. "*Nein*, just a visit," she said shortly. She turned to busy herself at the counter for a moment, and he got the distinct impression she was using the opportunity to compose herself. "Well, I'll leave you to enjoy your meal. Don't worry about the dishes—I'll do them tomorrow. You don't want to risk getting your cast wet, anyway. I'll be back around seven o'clock tomorrow morning, if that works for you."

"*Ja*. And, Miriam...*danke*." The expression felt awkward to say.

She gave him a neutral smile, patted the dog and departed.

Belly full with his first home-cooked meal in recent memory, he leaned back in his single kitchen chair and absently petted Major. What was it about Miriam that seemed to bring peace and ease? He didn't know.

But why was she here in Montana at all? He didn't know that either...but he wanted to.

Chapter Four

"You put this together for me?" Miriam pressed a hand to her chest, astounded.

"Ja." Her brother grinned with shy pleasure. "It wasn't being used, so I fixed it up a bit. We would have invited you to sleep in it yesterday, but Emma had a few last-minute touches she wanted to add."

Standing before them was a shed that had been transformed into a tiny guest cottage, painted brown with forest green trim. Pots of flowers and herbs were scattered around the miniature porch, on which a wooden rocking chair sat.

"Come inside," invited Thomas. He opened the cheerful forest green door and stepped inside.

Miriam followed, then stopped on the threshold with a gasp. "It's lovely!"

Though tiny, it had everything one needed for comfort: a miniature kitchen, a bathroom, a comfortable sitting area and—beyond full-length curtains—a tiny bedroom. A wall clock was centered over the open door, and its ticking was a comforting sound. Some of the added flourishes—muslin curtains at the windows, a small vase of wildflowers and a generous sampler of handmade soaps—had clearly been done by her sister-in-law.

Miriam felt tears prickling her eyes. It wasn't just the charm of the little guest house; it was the love and care behind it. Two years ago, her brother had been on the verge of being a criminal. Today he had a respectable job, a beautiful wife and stepdaughter, a child of his own on the way—and now he was offering her shelter made by his own hands.

She turned and hugged Thomas, overwhelmed with the goodness of *Gott*. "*Danke*," she whispered.

She knew he felt the same when he wrapped his arms around her. He pulled back after a moment, and she saw a suspicious sheen in his eyes. "You were the only one who believed in me during my worst days," he told her. "This is just a small way to pay you back. It's yours as long as you want to stay here."

She gave a shaky laugh. "With something this pretty, I may never leave."

"You may not want to. I think you'll find Montana will grow on you. I know I love it here. Can't imagine living anywhere else." He glanced at the clock over the doorway. "I have to get to work, so I'll leave you to explore."

Miriam knew her brother worked as a bookkeeper three days a week in town and two days a week in his little home office on the property, another retrofitted shed.

"But it's Saturday," she said. "Do you have so much work that your Saturdays are full?"

"Sometimes." He smiled the smile of a satisfied man.

"My business has grown over the past year. I'm now doing bookkeeping for most of the Plain businesses in the community. It allows me to provide for my family, including the *boppli* Emma will be having in a couple of months. *Gott ist gut, ja?*"

"*Ja*," said Miriam softly. Her eyes prickled. She was so proud of her *bruder*, it was difficult to say more.

After Thomas left, Miriam spent a few minutes looking into corners and cabinets. The tiny cabin had everything she could possibly need, including a miniature woodstove that would keep the space warm during cold weather. An empty floor-to-ceiling bookshelf was wedged along one wall. Miriam smiled. Her brother knew she was fond of her books.

A basket near the sink held a variety of soaps. She lifted one of the bars to her nose and sniffed. Lemon. Her sister-in-law was well known in town for her superb soaps.

She couldn't wait to move in. She walked the hundred feet to Thomas and Emma's cabin and knocked, then entered.

"What do you think?" inquired Emma with a smile.

"It's absolutely stunning." Miriam gave Emma a huge smile of her own. "And I understand I have you to thank for so many of the homey touches."

Emma laughed. "Perhaps a few. You have no idea how excited Thomas was to have you come stay with us. He's so grateful for your support during—during his past. Here, sit down. I've just got some quiche ready for lunch. After you've eaten, I'll help you move in."

"You'll do nothing of the sort." Miriam chuckled as she seated herself at the kitchen table, where little Hannah was engaged in drawing with crayons. "Not in your condition. Seven months, you said?"

"*Ja*. But I'm healthy as a horse, so don't feel like you have to coddle me." With her hands encased in oven mitts, Emma removed a sizzling quiche from the oven.

After a silent blessing, Miriam took a bite of the quiche and tasted broccoli, onions, bacon and cheese. "*Wunderbar*," she pronounced.

"*Danke*. It's a matter of pride to cook as much as we can with our own ingredients."

"You made the Swiss cheese?" exclaimed Miriam, impressed.

Emma chuckled. "*Oll recht*, the cheese is the exception. Aaron made that. He's the best cheese-maker in the area."

"So some of the milk I got this morning will become future cheese." Miriam took another bite. "He'll be giving me a crash course in cheese-making since I know it's part of his livelihood."

"He also tinkers," Emma added. "He's a clever fellow, always coming up with gadgets. How are you two getting along?" Emma poured some milk for Hannah.

"About as well as you'd expect." Miriam shrugged to indicate ambivalence. "You weren't kidding about his grumpiness. I'm trying to attribute it to any lingering pain from the broken arm rather than to just being a grumpy man."

"*Ja*, he's always been that way, as long as we've known him. I gather he had some sort of tragedy in his past, above and beyond whatever scarred his face."

"How did the accident happen, do you know?"

"*Nein*. He won't talk about it. It's understandable, I

suppose. Ooh." Emma paused and spread her hands over her belly, her eyes closed. Then she opened her eyes and grinned. "Active little fellow. He likes to kick."

"A sign of a *gut* healthy pregnancy."

"I was hoping you could deliver the baby when the time comes."

"Oh, Emma..." Miriam laid down her fork. "I don't know about that."

"I don't understand why you intend to give up nursing, Miriam. What will you do, if that's not an option?"

"Take care of Aaron's farm, for the moment." Miriam pushed the remaining quiche around her plate. She admired her sister-in-law's forthright manner, but right now her decision to leave nursing was still too tender, too new. "I have no other plans. In fact, there's a—a sort of void inside me, an empty spot that used to be filled with the passion of delivering babies and helping people heal."

Emma chewed her food thoughtfully. "Is the loss of one patient so great that you'd throw away years of training?"

"I—I don't know." Miriam toyed with her fork. "All I know is, I seem to have lost confidence in my own skills."

"I wonder..." Emma sliced herself another piece of quiche. "What would it take to become a licensed midwife in Montana? Perhaps you can just work here in the community, delivering babies."

Miriam tried to keep her voice gentle. "*Nein.* I've made a promise to *Gott*, remember? I'll—I'll find other work."

Emma sighed. "Can't blame me for trying. It just seems like a shame to waste all that lovely talent."

Miriam forced herself to finish the rest of the quiche, but the food was tasteless in her mouth. It *did* seem like a shame...but a promise was a promise.

After lunch, Miriam moved her suitcases and possessions to the little cabin and spent a couple of hours settling in, charmed with her cozy little home. But she was unable to shake off Emma's comment. Was it true? Was she wasting her talent by giving up her profession?

But how could she continue practicing nursing and midwifery when she had erred so badly as to lose not just one patient but two? The incident still weighed heavily on Miriam's conscience.

"Pretty!" said Hannah from the doorway.

Miriam turned and saw her little step-niece. "I think so too," she said. "It's like a doll's house, isn't it?"

"Ja." Hannah walked inside, her dark brown eyes taking in everything. "*Daed* built it for you."

"Your *daed* is a nice man for doing this. So is your *mamm*. You'll have to have tea here with me one day, *ja*?"

"Ja!" The child's eyes shone.

Moving slowly, Emma followed her daughter into the cottage. "Looks like you've settled in nicely."

"*Ja*, I wanted to get everything finished before I run into town for errands and then go over to Aaron's." Miriam hugged herself. "This is such a charming place. Thank you for putting it together for me."

"The only downside is it's rather small," commented Emma, resting one hand on her distended middle. "So you're to treat our house as your own. No need to knock or stand on ceremony. This kitchen is quite tiny, so anytime you feel like sharing a meal or cooking something more elaborate, you're welcome to use my kitchen."

"I see why my brother married you," replied Miriam, warmed by her sister-in-law's generous nature. "You're every bit as wonderful as he described."

Emma's eyes softened. "I'm so lucky to have him."

The other woman's obvious happiness gave Miriam a pinprick of longing. Would she ever have someone she could love as much as her sister-in-law obviously loved her brother? Miriam turned away to fiddle with the basket of sweet-smelling soaps on the counter.

"Well." She turned back. "I'm going to take advantage of still having my car and go into town for groceries to stock up my little kitchen here. Do you need anything?"

"*Nein*, but *danke*." Emma eyed her. "Is it true you intend to sell your car?"

"*Ja*. And my phone too. It's my goal to become baptized. I won't need those things in my life anymore."

Nodding, Emma said, "We have our own horse and buggy now, so if you ever need to use it, don't hesitate to ask."

"Danke."

A short while later, Miriam drove into town and parked in the small parking lot, wondering if she would get funny looks, being an Amish woman driving a car. But no one paid attention to her, except to give cursory glances at her *kapp*. As she wandered the store, stocking her cart with groceries, she thought about what Aaron might be lacking at his cabin and what she might be making him for meals. She added a few more items.

She might be unmoored at the moment, but at least she had something concrete to focus on: making sure Aaron was comfortable and his farm and animals were well cared for.

It was better than nothing.

"C'mon, you big goofus," said Aaron to Major. "I know you want to go for a swim."

Unable to perform his usual midday barn chores with one arm, Aaron had decided to take his dog to the pond and let the giant Newfoundland indulge in his love of water.

Major darted ahead with enthusiasm, and Aaron grinned. He'd gotten the dog as a puppy shortly after arriving in Montana two and a half years ago, and the animal was everything Aaron had hoped for: intelligent, tremendously strong, loyal and calm.

And big. The dog had topped out at a massive 160 pounds—a true gentle giant. In his self-imposed isolation, Major was his constant companion who never judged him.

The pond was a cattle pond—built to water livestock—and was fed by an underground spring. A grove of tall conifers shaded one side. Aaron had placed a solitary chair near the edge under the shade of the trees and kept a floating toy under the chair.

"Go on, then. Go get it!" Aaron flung the floatie into the water, and Major crashed after it, swimming out to seize and "rescue" it. Aaron knew Newfoundland dogs had an instinctive desire to perform water rescues, and he saw no harm in encouraging the activity.

For an hour, he threw the plaything into the water,

and Major brought it back each time. Finally, the animal seemed to be tiring, and Aaron suspected Miriam might be arriving shortly, so he called Major out of the water, waited until the dog had shaken most of the water from his coat and headed back toward the cabin.

His energy dissipated, Major padded calmly next to Aaron as they approached the cabin, his tongue hanging out. Aaron smiled at him. What an amazing animal he was…

"You should smile more often."

Aaron gasped. There stood Miriam, next to a tree near the cabin, apparently waiting for him. A shaft of sunlight pierced the branches, lighting up her *kapp* and illuminating her honey-colored hair. She had a gentle smile on her face.

Despite her jaw-dropping beauty, Aaron felt vulnerable being caught in a private moment with his dog. Since the accident, he seldom smiled at people, reserving his affection for his animals, who returned it wholeheartedly. At her words, he felt his face stiffen and resume its usual appearance.

"*Guder nammidaag*," he said. "Are you here for the evening chores?" At the obvious question, he felt his face heat. *Of course* she was there for the evening chores.

"*Ja*," she replied. When Major padded up to her, she gave the dog a tentative pat. "You're wet, big guy," she told him. "Come back when all that fur has dried."

"I took him swimming," explained Aaron.

She looked surprised. "Where?"

"I have a stock pond over there." He pointed. "Newfies love water, and with all that fur, it's helpful to let him cool down once in a while."

She nodded. "You're so *gut* with animals, Aaron. And they all love you too."

"Well, I have to have *some* redeeming qualities, don't I?" he retorted.

Rather than lose her temper, she only chuckled. "I'll go tackle the barn chores, and when I finish, I can make butter from yesterday's cream."

Already she was adapting to his schedule of chores. Temporarily incapacitated as he was, he didn't know what he would do without her willingness to work in his stead.

He watched her slim figure as she made her way toward the barn. Then he entered the cabin.

He puttered about, trying to do things one-handed. He removed a gallon jar from the icebox and began ladling the cream into a double boiler pot, which he placed on the propane stove. He slipped a kitchen thermometer into the cream and began gently heating and stirring. Cream turned to butter much more easily at room temperature, and he usually sped up the process by using the stove.

But pouring the warmed cream into the sterilized glass butter churn required two hands. He would have to wait for Miriam for that chore.

She came in from the barn a few minutes later, carrying a basket of eggs. "*Oll recht*, the cows are all set for the night, the calves are locked in the calf pen, everyone has fresh water and the chicken coop is clean. The only thing I didn't do was lock the hens in for the night, since it's too early."

"*Danke. Vielen dank*," he told her.

She washed her hands at the sink and eyed the double boiler on the stove. "Is that the cream ready to churn?"

"*Ja.*"

"I'll take care of it."

Aaron stepped back and watched her bustling efficiency as she transferred the warmed cream to the oversize glass jar, then fitted the lid with the built-in paddles operated by a hand crank. He usually churned butter twice a week, and she hadn't done this task before, so how…

"You've done this before," he observed as she screwed on the lid and began turning the handle.

"*Ja*, of course. I was raised making butter." She brought the churn over to the kitchen table, which was more suited to her height, and commenced the task of turning the handle. "So guess what?"

"What?" He was surprised at the impish smile she wore, as if she possessed a secret.

"My brother showed me where I'll be staying. He took a shed and outfitted it as a complete little guest cabin. Can you imagine?"

"Is that the shed out behind their house?"

"*Ja.*"

"I thought I saw him doing some work on it," he said, recalling the times he'd heard the sounds of hammer and saw. "But I had no idea what he was doing."

"He made it just for me. Oh, Aaron, you should see it. It's the most darling little cottage…"

He watched her as she chattered on about the amenities of her new home. Her eyes sparkled, her teeth flashed in a smile as she talked about the cabin. "He even built me a floor-to-ceiling bookshelf!" she concluded with a grin. "Thomas knows I'm a great reader. I don't have a collection of books quite as impressive as yours, but I brought all my books with me."

Aaron said very little. He was too lost in admiration for her lively beauty, still unable to believe such an attractive woman wasn't repulsed by his simple presence. Like Denise…

"…cheese?"

He snapped himself back to reality. "I'm sorry, what did you say?"

"I said, is tomorrow the day you want to show me how to make cheese?"

"*Nein*, tomorrow is Sunday. But I'll need to on Monday. I have to keep up with the milk production—especially this time of year, when the cows are producing heavily—or the milk will go to waste."

"Emma made a quiche today for lunch with Swiss cheese she said you'd made. It was delicious."

"*Danke.* Swiss takes a while to age, so I have a special root cellar where I keep it."

"What other cheese do you make?" Miriam asked as she continued to turn the handle of the churn.

"Cheddar, mozzarella, cream cheese, Swiss and Parmesan. Those are my specialties."

"And you sell them at the Yoders' store in town?"

"Ja."

"How often do you bring the fresh cheese in?"

"I don't. Another lady in the community brings them in for me."

She turned a surprised face to him. "Why?"

"'Why' what?"

"Why don't you bring the cheese in to the store yourself?"

He turned away. "I don't go into town."

"At all?" Her voice scaled up.

"At all."

At her sudden silence, he risked a glance at her. She wore a thoughtful, calculated expression.

"So you're hiding up here," she finally concluded, looking serious.

"*Ja*, of course. I'm surprised it took you so long to realize that."

"Aaron, you must know that's not healthy."

"It's none of your business," he retorted. "I've had my fill of *Englischers* who do nothing but stare."

"*Ja*, perhaps, but how can you expect them to get used to you if you don't show your face?"

He pierced her with a hard look. "If you went from beautiful to ugly, would *you* willingly expose yourself to whispers and avoided glances?"

"I don't know." She cocked her head. "It would be a challenge, to be sure. So...you intend to spend the rest of your life hiding on your farm and never seeing another soul?"

"I see everyone at church twice a month."

"That's a start," she murmured, then gave him a sunny smile that weakened his knees. "This is done." She stopped cranking the churn handle. "Now, where's your paddle? I need to start rinsing the butter."

He wondered about the abrupt change in subject. For a brief moment, he had bared his soul—and she talked of butter? It confirmed his opinion that no one could really, truly understand his current situation, the trauma he felt, the isolation.

He took a deep breath. It wasn't Miriam's fault, and she was just the latest in a long line of people who couldn't understand what it was like to live as a "beast."

"The butter paddle is here," he growled, fishing the implement out of a kitchen drawer.

She took the curved wooden paddle most Amish used to press the buttermilk out of fresh butter. "But I'll wait to finish the butter until I make you dinner."

"'Dinner'?"

"*Ja*, you eat dinner, don't you?" She opened a cupboard and looked inside, tapping her chin while considering the contents. "I could make you a hash brown casserole. Would you like that?"

What would it take to scare her off? Aaron didn't know. He only knew he was grudgingly impressed by her determination to do what she saw as her duty to care for him during his recovery.

"Hash brown casserole sounds *gut*," he admitted, and he watched as she got to work.

Chapter Five

Miriam opened her eyes, momentarily confused as to where she was. Instead of the sterile white ceiling of her apartment in Indiana, she was in the cozy bedroom in her little cabin. She hugged herself with delight. The woodwork around her was Plain—as it should be—but through her open window, she could hear birdsong and saw the sun was just rising. Already, she liked it here in Montana.

Suddenly filled with energy, she threw off the blankets and got dressed. Today was a church Sunday, and it would be her first church service in her new community. She had to get Aaron's chores finished before she could clean herself up and get ready. But first, she had to fetch the work gloves she'd left in Thomas and Emma's house.

She walked toward the house. Stepping quietly into their kitchen, she expected everyone to still be asleep. But her sister-in-law was awake and busy. The kitchen smelled of frying bacon.

"*Guder mariye*," Emma said in a low voice as she stirred something on the stove. "Are you off to Aaron's?"

"*Ja*. I'm guessing it will take me an hour to get his chores done. Then I'll come back and clean up for church."

"Tell Aaron if he wants a ride to the service, we have room in the buggy." Emma smiled and patted her midsection. "Thomas doesn't want me to waddle all the way to church. Says it takes too long."

Miriam chuckled. "What time should I tell him?"

"Around eight-thirty. The service starts at nine."

"I'll let him know." Miriam snatched the work gloves she'd forgotten yesterday and headed for the door.

The morning was fresh and sunny. Miriam breathed in the pine-scented air. So far she very much liked what she saw in this western part of the state. The air lacked Indiana's typical humidity, and it smelled fresh and clean.

She bypassed Aaron's house and went straight to the barn. The chores were becoming routine now, and she was pleased the cows responded to her calmly as she set about milking them. She kept her pace quick and efficient, and by the time the chores were finished, the sun was properly up. She carefully poured the buckets of milk into the milk can, strapped it onto the hand truck and carted it up to the house.

She found Aaron awake and sipping a cup of coffee in the kitchen. He had a clean, Sunday look about him, with his brown hair neatly combed and a fresh shirt on. *"Guder mariye."*

"Guder mariye." She heaved the milk onto the counter. "Emma invited you to ride to the church service with us in their buggy, if you want. Since your arm is no doubt still aching, I thought you might want to accept."

There was surprise in his eyes, then wariness. She

could almost see the battle warring within him. "I don't think I should..."

She began the process of straining the milk. "You know, Aaron, the offer was meant to be neighborly. There's a fine line between independence and stubbornness. It would be a kindness to accept."

He scowled, the expression somehow magnifying the scars on his face. "Fine. I'll accept."

She laughed. "*Gut.* Emma said they'll be leaving around eight-thirty." She put the strained milk in the icebox. "See you then."

Walking back to her brother's property, she wondered how often Aaron avoided seeing even the people within his own church. Surely he realized the fastest way for any group to accept his appearance was to be seen as often as possible? She knew his approach—to hide himself on his farm, to avoid all but the most necessary human contact—was unhealthy. She wondered what it would take to pull him out of his shell.

Miriam ate breakfast with her brother and his wife, then hurried back to her cabin to dress for church. By the time Thomas had the horse hitched to the buggy, Miriam was wondering if Aaron would back out of the offer to ride to church. But no. There he was, walking up the driveway, a wary expression on his face as if he expected to be rebuffed.

"*Guder mariye*, Aaron," Thomas called out. "Beautiful morning, *ja*?"

"*Ja.* Um...*guder mariye.*" Aaron's eyes darted from Emma to Hannah to Miriam. "*Danke* for the offer of a ride."

"I can't have Emma walking that far in her condition," confirmed Thomas, who turned to his wife. "Ready, *lieb*?"

"*Ja.* Aaron, would you mind putting this basket in the back?" Emma handed Aaron a hamper containing lunch.

Miriam almost laughed at the expression on Aaron's face. To be included in the casual request was clearly not what he'd expected. How long had it been since he'd involved himself in ordinary family activities? Years, she suspected.

Thomas assisted Emma into the buggy, then lifted Hannah onto her lap. Miriam found herself in the back with Aaron.

Curious, little Hannah peered over Emma's shoulder and stared at Aaron. At first, Miriam was concerned the child's blatant inquisitiveness might make Aaron even more self-conscious. She was just about to say something when suddenly, the child held out a cloth toy to the silent man. "See my doll?" she said.

Aaron awkwardly took the faceless traditional-Amish plaything. "It's very nice," he said. "What's her name?"

"Elizabeth."

"She's pretty." He handed the doll back to the child.

Hannah took her toy and faced forward, and Thomas directed the buggy toward the road.

Miriam stole a glance at Aaron. He had a bewildered expression on his face, and she could almost guess his thoughts. Here was a child who had *not* recoiled in horror from his face but merely offered to let him see her toy. Silently, Miriam blessed the little girl.

The trip to the farm where the church service was being hosted took just a few minutes. A flow of people—

some walking, some in buggies—made their way to the farm in an increasing tide. Thomas pulled the horse to a halt and jumped out of the buggy. A young man came over and began unhitching the animal. Thomas turned to assist Emma and Hannah. Aaron, too, jumped out and courteously offered a hand to Miriam.

She raised her eyebrows at the gallantry; then primly she nodded her thanks, laid her hand in his and descended from the buggy. She wondered how long it had been since he'd had a chance to perform the polite gesture. For that matter, how long had it been since he'd *wanted* to perform the polite gesture.

Walking in beside Emma and Hannah, Miriam was aware of the sharpened glances from curious people, both men and women alike. Being new in the community, she expected it. But no one offered introductions. Socialization happened after the church service, not before. She stepped into the large, clean barn where the service was being held and took a seat on the bench next to Emma on the women's side.

"Here, why don't you sit in my lap?" she asked Hannah. "Your *mamm* has a baby inside her now, and it makes her lap smaller."

"*Ja*," agreed Hannah.

Miriam drew the child up and snaked her arms around her little body. It felt good to hold a child. Someday she hoped to hold one of her own.

The bishop stood up to begin. Miriam hadn't met the church leader yet, though she knew he was Emma's uncle and lived just a short distance away. He was lanky and had a wispy beard, but despite his air of quiet authority, his eyes were kind.

The service proceeded as usual: hymns, an introductory sermon, prayers, scripture readings, the bishop's sermon, testimonies and then closing prayers.

Just before the ending of the service, the bishop introduced her as Thomas Kemp's sister, and mentioned her medical training in passing. Emma rose, acknowledged the greeting, then sat back down. Part of her wished the bishop hadn't mentioned her experience as a midwife, but it was too late now.

When it came time to go outdoors and prepare for the meal, Miriam found herself surrounded by well-wishers from the women's side.

"*Guder nammidaag*," said a pretty young matron, heavy with pregnancy. "My name is Eva Hostettler."

"I'm Mabel Yoder."

"I'm Abigail Troyer."

"I'm Ruth Chupp."

"I'm Lois Beiler."

Miriam laughed at the outpouring of warm welcome. *"Danke!"* she said to everyone. "It's so nice to meet you. Please forgive me if I don't remember your names at first..."

She received invitations to tea, to quilting bees, to canning parties. She thanked everyone and accepted what invitations she could without feeling she was jeopardizing her work at Aaron's.

The initial flurry of greetings died down as people began lining up for the midday meal. Miriam followed Emma to the tables laden with food to fill her plate. Hannah had run off to play with some friends.

"What a nice group of people," she told her sister-in-law.

"*Ja*, they are. It's a very welcoming community. Oh, by the way, my *onkel* would like to know if you would have time to meet with him this week. He always likes to get to know newcomers."

"*Ja*, sure, I'd be happy to..."

From the corner of her eye, she noticed Aaron standing alone, apparently waiting for the crowds to thin at the food tables before filling his own plate.

Even in the midst of the camaraderie—from which, Aaron was by no means excluded—he seemed alone. Other men engaged him in conversation, no one avoided him and everyone seemed to welcome him—but still, he seemed alone.

Impulsively, she caught his eye and jerked her head toward one of the picnic tables while holding her plate aloft. She hoped he understood the gesture as an invitation to join the Kemp family for the meal.

What happened next absolutely staggered her. Aaron smiled. Not just any smile—a beautiful smile that transformed his face and made it glow. She realized that beneath those scars was an extraordinarily handsome man. Did he even know that?

She wondered what it would take to get him to smile more.

Aaron watched Miriam become surrounded by people after the church service. While he was glad to see her welcomed so warmly, it further drew a line between them. No one had ever welcomed him, even when he'd first arrived. He knew he couldn't turn his back on *Gott* and refuse to attend church services, but even among his fellow church members, it took a while to be accepted.

No, that wasn't correct. He'd always been *accepted* here—he just didn't have close friends.

But watching Miriam talking to the other women, he knew that wouldn't be her fate. She seemed to have a knack for friendship. He didn't. Not anymore, at least.

He turned away and saw something that hit him like a blow to his stomach: it wasn't just the women who were clustering around Miriam—some of the younger unmarried men were watching her from afar. He saw one group of older teen boys gathered together, talking and casting glances at the newcomer.

She wouldn't be single for long; of that, he was certain. A pretty, eligible woman like Miriam would be snapped up by some lucky man, and that would be that. He'd politely sit through the marriage ceremony and wish her well, then return to his solitary existence with only his dog for a companion. He had no hope of ever getting married, especially to someone like her.

Even as people ebbed and flowed around him, getting ready for the post-church potluck meal, he felt isolated. And lonely. Families mingled, children darted around, laughter bubbled up from various groups—but he was alone. Always alone.

He glanced at Miriam, who was standing in line near her brother and sister-in-law. She caught his eye, jerked her head toward the picnic tables and held up her plate with a questioning look.

The message couldn't be clearer: *Come eat lunch with us.*

Aaron felt like a fifty-pound weight had been lifted from his shoulders. Impulsively, he smiled at her, a smile of relief and thanks and appreciation that she had noticed him.

Her eyebrows shot up, and her own smile widened.

Aaron had a purpose now, if only for the next hour or so. He joined the line for food, behind a man named Adam Chupp, one of the church's best carpenters.

"How's the arm feeling?" asked Adam, giving him a sympathetic look. "I heard you had an accident."

"*Ja*, Miriam Kemp accidentally hit me with her car during that thunderstorm last week." He lifted his cast. "Not easy to milk cows like this, I can assure you."

Adam cocked his head and regarded Aaron's arm. "*Gut* point," he affirmed. "How *do* you milk your cows with one arm?"

He took a step forward as the food line advanced. "Actually, Miriam's doing most of the heavy work for me," Aaron admitted. "She says it's because she feels guilty for injuring me, but I think it's because she came out here without a job in mind and needs something to do. Regardless, I'm grateful."

"You're the inventor, ain't so?" quipped Adam. "You need to invent a one-handed milking machine." He picked up a plate and began filling it.

Aaron stood still, momentarily transfixed. It was true he had a knack for invention. Could he come up with some technique to milk cows one-handed? He knew a fair number of older people from his old community in Pennsylvania who'd had to give up milking when it became too painful due to arthritis or some other condition. What if…?

"You're next," said a quiet voice behind him.

"Sorry," he said to the teen boy. He picked up a plate

and braced it between his chest and his arm cast, then began spooning food onto it.

When the plate was full, he made his way over to the table where the Kemp family was dining. "May I join you?" he asked.

"*Ja*, of course." Emma scooted over to give him room, and Aaron found himself seated opposite Miriam.

"Looks like you couldn't juggle a drink along with your plate," she observed. "Want me to get you something?"

"A lemonade, if you wouldn't mind."

"*Ja*, sure. Back in a moment." She swung off the picnic bench and headed toward the buffet.

"How's the arm feeling?" Thomas asked.

"Still a bit sore," Aaron admitted. "I'm trying not to take pain pills, but sometimes I need to." He added quietly, "I have a fairly high tolerance for pain now." After three months of recovery in the hospital after the fire, pain was all too familiar.

Thomas nodded as if understanding the deeper meaning. "I'm glad Miriam was available to help out. But keep in mind, if you need something heavier done, don't hesitate to ask. That's what neighbors are for."

"Danke." Aaron took a bite of macaroni and cheese and reflected on how fortunate he was to live across the road from the Kemps. They had always been good neighbors.

Miriam returned with a glass in her hand. "Here you are."

"Danke." He tried not to stare at her as she reseated herself. Everything about her seemed bathed in a golden light, from her honey-colored hair to the glow of her

skin. Or perhaps it was just an overactive imagination, the product of a lonely mind.

He dropped his gaze to his plate. Back in Pennsylvania, Denise—the woman he had been betrothed to—had recoiled from him after the accident. In some ways, her rejection had left deeper scars than the fire.

Miriam had never seen him the way he used to be. He had no hope that she could see under the scars to the lonely man beneath.

He took a deep and silent breath and refocused on the conversation between Thomas and Miriam.

"There's a lady who has a business making dolls," Thomas was saying. "She's an older woman, widowed, staying with her sister and husband. She's mentioned she might be interested in hiring out parts of the assembly process, if you're looking for work."

Miriam shook her head and glanced at Aaron. "Maybe once he gets back on his feet," she told her brother. "What did the doctor say, Aaron, about when your cast would come off?"

"About seven weeks."

"Then that's how long I should wait before looking for paid employment," she said to Thomas.

Her brother smiled. "Fair enough."

"Aaron, if you have any more Swiss cheese for sale, I'd be interested," said Emma. "It's one of my favorites, and I don't know anyone who makes it better than you."

"I have a fair bit in storage in the root cellar," he replied. "It takes a long time to age, but I have some three-month-old blocks that are just about ready."

"Ja, bitte." She chuckled. "In my state, I could probably eat an entire block for breakfast."

"You're eating for two," said Thomas, smiling at his wife.

Aaron had no idea how pregnancy affected a woman's appetite, but he enjoyed the gentle interactions within the Kemp family.

"What work do you plan to do tomorrow?" Miriam asked him. "Did you say cheese-making was on the agenda?"

"*Ja*," he replied. "The icebox is swimming in milk. The best way to take care of the excess is by making cheese. I try to keep to a schedule, and this week I planned to make a lot of cheddar. I'll need to walk you through the steps."

"I have to warn you, I only watched *Mamm* make cheese when I was a little girl but never made any myself, so I'm completely new to this," Miriam told him before she took a bite of potato salad.

Aaron was silent for a moment, then said, "Miriam… if I haven't mentioned it recently, *danke* for getting me through this."

She raised her eyebrows. "As I've said before, I feel responsible to help you run your farm until you're able. Besides, it keeps me busy."

The bishop approached Miriam. "I haven't introduced myself," he said, offering his hand. "I'm Bishop Samuel Beiler."

Miriam stood up and shook his hand. "How do you do? I'm Miriam Kemp, Thomas's *schwester*. Emma said you wanted to meet with me."

"*Ja*. Just a casual meeting. Would tomorrow afternoon work for you?"

"I don't know. I'm working for Aaron at the moment,

and he said we're making cheese tomorrow." She turned to him. "Is it an all-day project?"

"*Ja*, pretty much," he replied. "It usually takes me from morning to evening chores to finish everything."

"What about today?" she persisted.

He shrugged. "It's Sunday. Except for chores, I'm not doing any other work."

Miriam turned back to the church leader. "Would this afternoon work for you?"

"*Ja, gut*," he replied. "Three o'clock?"

"Three o'clock," she affirmed.

Miriam sat back down as the bishop walked away. "What's he like?" she asked Aaron. "The bishop?"

"You should ask her," Aaron replied, nodding toward Emma. "She's his niece."

"That means I'm biased." Emma smiled. "Go on. Give her your own impression."

"He's fair," Aaron replied promptly. "A *gut* church leader, well respected." He traced a pattern on his plate with his fork. "This community is something of a ragtag collection of church members from all over the country. Many of us have left painful things behind and settled here for a fresh start. He's in a position where he has to balance all these different pasts and influences against the rules of the *Ordnung*." He raised his eyes to her and saw sympathy in them. "For that, I respect him."

"Amen," said Thomas, his voice heartfelt.

"So you left something behind, did you?" Miriam asked softly.

"*Ja*." But Aaron wasn't ready to talk about that. He forestalled any further questioning by standing up and gathering his plate and cutlery, using his unbroken arm awkwardly. He nodded to Thomas. "I think I'm fine walking back alone. *Danke* for the ride in this morning."

He walked away before Thomas could answer. He knew he had acted rudely, but he didn't know how else to evade Miriam's painful question about what he'd left behind.

He deposited his dishes in a bin and, without saying a word to anyone, slipped away from the gathering to walk home alone.

What he'd left behind in Pennsylvania was a man. It was a beast who had settled here in Montana.

Chapter Six

Miriam drove home with her brother and his family in their buggy, thinking about Aaron's rude departure from the after-church potluck. It was obvious there was something extraordinarily painful in his past, and her instincts told her it wasn't just the accident that had scarred his face; something had scarred his heart as well. She wondered if he would ever allow himself to heal from it.

"There's Uncle Samuel's home." Emma pointed to a house just a short distance away from the Kemps' own farm. "You can easily walk there."

"I think I met your aunt in passing," remarked Miriam. "It was right after the church service was over, but there were so many people introducing themselves, it was all a blur."

"Well, you'll see her again. She's very nice."

"*Tante* Lois and I make cookies!" announced Hannah from her seat in back next to Miriam.

"What's your favorite kind?" Miriam asked her niece.

The child thought for a moment. "Chocolate chip," she finally announced.

"That's my favorite too. We should make some one day."

"Today?"

Miriam chuckled at the girl's eagerness. "*Nein, liebling.* I have a meeting with your uncle Samuel this afternoon. But soon—I promise."

"As for me, I'm taking a nap," announced Emma, yawning. "I find myself tiring more easily in the afternoon."

"Then Hannah and I will read stories in the hammock," replied Thomas, smiling over his shoulder at his stepdaughter. "That's one of our favorite things to do when your *mamm* is napping, ain't so?"

It was all Miriam could do to keep from tearing up from sheer joy at her brother's happiness. After a lifetime of being a troublemaker, he was now a solid family man. It was clear Hannah adored him as well.

She sighed, wondering what her own future held.

Shortly before three o'clock that afternoon, she made sure her *kapp* and apron were neat, then set off for the bishop's house. The afternoon was warm, and she was glad the distance wasn't far.

The bishop's home turned out to be a barn that had been renovated into a cozy house. Her brother had mentioned that, due to the newness of the settlement, most older people didn't have the option of living in the traditional *daadi haus* behind an adult child's farmhouse. Privately, she suspected that as the bishop and his wife aged, Thomas and Emma would soon find themselves building such a structure onto their own land for Emma's *tante* and *onkel.*

But for the moment, the Beilers seemed strong and able to handle a small farm. There was a large garden, some young fruit trees, a chicken coop and yard, and what looked like a pigpen.

She knocked on the front door. Within moments, it was whisked open by Lois Beiler. "Come in, child, come in!" Lois was short and plump, with graying hair and twinkling eyes.

"Danke." Now that Miriam was seeing Lois again, she remembered their brief introduction a few hours ago after the church service. "What a lovely farm you have."

Lois chuckled. "Sometimes it gets beyond me, but Emma is a big help. Surprisingly, so is little Hannah, especially in the garden. The child adores growing things."

The bishop emerged from an inside room. "*Guder nammidaag, guder nammidaag,*" he rumbled with a smile. "Would you like a glass of iced tea?"

"*Ja*, sure. *Danke.*" Miriam wasn't thirsty but didn't want to be rude.

He poured two glasses from a pitcher in the ice box, then led the way toward a back office outfitted with plain oak furniture. "Have a seat."

"What a beautiful cat." Miriam patted a gorgeous calico snoozing in a basket on the bishop's desk. The animal lifted its head and blinked at her.

"*Ja*, this is Thomasina. She's my favorite pet." As the bishop seated himself, the cat climbed out of her basket and onto the bishop's lap. Her loud purring filled the room as he scratched under her chin.

Miriam decided a man whose cat clearly loved him must be a good man.

"So..." The bishop sipped his iced tea. "What brings you out here to Montana? Is it just to visit your brother?"

Miriam felt the familiar weight of guilt descending

on her shoulders. "I left the church to study nursing. In my mind, I never left my faith behind, but I felt called to care for people and needed to get the right training. In Indiana, I'm a licensed EMT, a registered nurse and registered midwife. Everything was going fine until I—I lost a maternity patient. It—it left me shaken, I guess you could say. When my *bruder*, Thomas, invited me to come stay with him and Emma for a while, I jumped at the chance to get away."

"It must have been very traumatic for you."

"It was." She stared blindly at the cat's empty basket. "I lost the confidence I had in my own skills. I never realized how important that was when it came to my work. Suddenly, everything seemed difficult, like trying to work while wading through molasses. I decided *Gott* was trying to push me back toward the church after my excursion into the *Englisch* world. So I've left my career behind." She met the older man's eyes. "It is my desire, Bishop Beiler, to become baptized and join the church."

"I see no problem with that goal," he said. "We have some people getting baptized in early November, so I'm starting classes next month for that group. But, Miriam, I would urge you to reconsider your goal of leaving behind your medical training. There is a need here for medical care, especially midwifery. My own niece mentioned that she'd love for you to deliver her baby."

Miriam felt her gut clench. Right now, at her first meeting with the church leader, she did not want to delve into her bargain with *Gott* to give up medicine if He would forgive her for her part in losing her patient. To have the bishop request that she become licensed here in Montana was something she hadn't expected.

"But… but…" she sputtered. "I—I can't. I just can't…"

"What do you plan to do, then?" inquired the bishop. His faded blue eyes were sympathetic. "You're leaving a lot behind—and while I'm grateful Thomas and Emma have a home for you, everyone needs a purpose in life."

"Well, right now I'm working for Aaron Lapp until he recovers from his injury."

The bishop waved a dismissive hand. "His recovery will take, what…another six or eight weeks? After that, he'll be back to his solitary existence and doubtless won't want anyone around. What will you do then?"

"I d-don't know…"

"Then that is what you must figure out." The older man offered her a gentle smile.

Miriam stared at him. What had at first seemed like unfair pressure to continue a career she had left behind had turned, in a heartbeat, into an open invitation to find an alternative.

"*Ja*," she said slowly. "I guess that's what I must do." She was impressed with the church leader's quiet wisdom.

"There's certainly no rush," he went on. "In fact, working on Aaron's farm might give you a *gut* opportunity to pause and reflect, and perhaps find your path—the path *Gott* wants you to be on."

"I have a lot of thinking to do," she acknowledged. The panic receded. He was right: there was no rush. "Thomas mentioned an older woman who has a sewing business making dolls and that she might need help doing piecework?"

"That would be Ruby Lapp. No relation to Aaron. *Ja*, she has a very nice business making traditional Amish dolls for a wholesaler. Her daughter-in-law back in Indiana started the business but got too busy to keep up. Now Ruby is working solo. I'm sure she could use the help, if you're inclined."

"Probably not until after Aaron no longer needs me to work his farm." She smiled. "It's good to have options. Meanwhile, I'm snug as a bug in the lovely little guest house Thomas built, and it's *gut* to be near family."

"Thomas has been a wonderful addition to the community," the bishop said. "You're more familiar than anyone with his rough past. He's always spoken so highly of you. It's a testament to *Gott*'s goodness to see what he's like today."

"Ja." Her face softened. "My baby *bruder* has grown up at last, and he couldn't have picked a better wife. I love Emma like a sister already."

"Well, it sounds like you're settling in nicely. I'm always available if you need any help or guidance. And my wife, Lois, always has an overabundance in her garden—so later in the summer, you're welcome to her fresh produce."

Miriam chuckled. "I love gardening as much as the next woman, but I'm awed by what Emma has done. Oh...one more thing. I have a car and a smart phone I'll be selling as soon as possible. I don't see the need to keep either."

The bishop smiled. "You'll fit in very well here, Miriam. Welcome to Pierce."

Miriam took the hint and rose to her feet, then shook the bishop's hand. "*Danke.* Well, I'd best get to Aaron's place to do the evening chores. Tomorrow I'll get a crash course in cheese-making."

"How are you two getting along? Aaron can be… prickly."

"*Ja*, he can. But that's one thing my nurses' training has prepared me for. It's easy to recognize shortness stemming from pain, and a broken arm is a painful thing."

"Well, it sounds like he has a good helper in you. *Danke* for coming today, Miriam."

Miriam walked back to her cabin in a thoughtful mood. Oddly it was Aaron on her mind, and the bishop's acknowledgment of the injured man's lonely existence. Did no one reach out to him?

She tucked the thought away. It might be worth discussing with Bishop Beiler at some point in the future.

Aaron stood next to his favorite cow, Matilda, and regarded her with interest. That morning, after church, Adam Chupp had joked that Aaron needed to invent a one-handed milking machine. What would be necessary to make such a device?

He looked at the cow and pondered…

"Is everything okay?" inquired Miriam from behind him. "You look so thoughtful."

He was only slightly startled since it was time for her evening barn chores.

"*Guder nammidaag*," he said. "Just thinking about something one of the men said after church today. He said I need to invent a one-handed milking device. I realize he's right. I was just looking at Matilda and considering how it might be done."

Miriam slipped out of her shoes and into the muck boots she now kept in the barn. "Oh, are you an inventor?" she half joked.

"Actually, *ja*."

She snapped her head up and stared. "You're kidding."

A touch of a smile quirked his lips. "No, I'm not. It's just a gift I have—the ability to solve problems. Most of what I've come up with are shortcuts for farm chores, and I offer them around the community, but this is a new challenge. A way to make it easier to milk cows could help people like me, who are temporarily incapacitated. But it could also help people with, say, arthritis or some other condition that makes milking too difficult."

"But how could you milk one-handed?" In her knee-high boots, Miriam clumped over to stand next to Matilda.

"I'm thinking there might be a way to make a device that creates a vacuum." He squatted down and pointed to the cow's udder. "Something like a handgrip or a lever that could create the vacuum and pull the milk out into…into a bottle or something."

Miriam stared at the cow for a few seconds. "Fascinating."

Aaron stood up and rested his cast on the cow's back, staring into the middle distance.

Miriam smiled. "I can almost see the gears turning in your brain. But how will you find the parts you need to create this device?"

He was brought back to the present. "There's a machinist in town," he replied. "I've worked with him before when it comes to making things. His specialty is metal, but metal would be too heavy for a milking device, so I'll talk to him about alternatives."

She shook her head and bestowed what almost seemed

like an admiring look upon him. "I don't know how you do it," she admitted. "I don't have the ability to solve problems like this." She turned to pluck out a hayfork and moved toward one of the stalls.

He watched her slim figure as she worked. She had her own gifts, he knew. One thing she seemed unaware of—or maybe it was just him—was the air of calmness she brought with her wherever she went. He, who had shunned all company for the last three years, actually found himself looking forward to having her on his farm. Even though she was doing anything but resting while she worked, there was something peaceful about her presence that he enjoyed.

Then he remembered something. "How did your meeting with the bishop go?"

"Oh." Her face fell. "Fine."

He managed a rusty chuckle. "That sounded like everything *but* fine."

"Well, if you must know, he wants me to continue with my nursing career here in Montana. Especially midwifery." Her expression looked cross.

He was puzzled. "What's wrong with that?"

Her expression immediately changed from angry to almost panicked. "I—I planned to leave it all behind." She pitched waste material into a wheelbarrow with unusual vigor.

He was even more puzzled. "I know you were a nurse, but that's all I know about it. Just how much medical training have you had?"

"A lot." She paused a moment and stared at the straw at her feet. "Well, you know I'm a registered nurse. But

I'm also a qualified EMT and a registered midwife. At least, I was in Indiana."

His jaw dropped. "You're kidding."

"*Nein.* It is—it *was*—my calling. I left the church for training. But I've given it all up now, and that's the end of the matter. I told the bishop I was eager to be baptized as soon as possible. He said I should be ready by November."

He kept his voice gentle. "That's a lot to give up."

"*Ja*, well, I made a big mistake and lost a patient and her baby. I can't forgive myself for that."

Instinctively, Aaron knew the short statement barely hinted at the scope of emotional trauma she was dealing with. One of the barn cats started winding itself around her boots, looking for affection, but she appeared not to see it. Instead, she gave a small shake of her head and continued cleaning the stall.

Just a few moments ago, Aaron had been reflecting on the air of calmness and peace she seemed to carry with her. That was gone. What he saw now was a woman tormented by loss—both medical and spiritual.

She finished the stalls with remarkable speed, then said, "I'll just nip out and do the chickens. I think that'll be it for the evening." After slipping out of her boots, she redonned her shoes. "I'll see you in the morning."

"Ja, gut. Danke." He watched as she left the barn and made her way toward the chicken coop with unnecessary haste. She clearly wanted to be left alone.

After his admittedly rude departure from the church potluck earlier that day, he understood completely. Sometimes it was necessary to be alone to deal with memories.

In a thoughtful frame of mind, he went back to the house, where Major romped around him with enthusiasm. He leaned down and tousled the fur on Major's head with affection. The huge dog gave him a goofy smile.

It seemed Miriam was scared to reenter the medical field after the traumatic loss she'd experienced. A thought crossed his mind: he was just as scared to reenter the matrimonial field. In many ways, they were similar. He often found himself wishing he could dip his toes back in the water and court someone, but he was afraid of rejection. The pain of it still stung.

Denise, the woman he had thought to marry, was herself long-since married and already had a child. His *mamm* had filled him in with the news in one of her letters.

He touched the scarring on his face and wondered if any woman would ever be able to look beyond it to the man beneath—the man he still felt himself to be.

There was one difference between him and Miriam. She could, presumably, overcome her fears and go back to nursing again. Yet he had no option but to live with his scarred face forever. It was a thought that never failed to press him down in despair.

Long ago he had railed at *Gott*, furious at what had befallen him. Why had this happened? Had *Gott* been angry at him? He'd thought he was living a decent, quiet life, following the *Ordnung*. He never got into trouble as a teen, not even on his *rumspringa*. What had he done to deserve such a fate? Why him? What did it mean? Was it supposed to be a lesson? He'd prayed over it, scoured his Bible, but no rational explanation had come to him.

Well, he'd gotten over his anger at *Gott*. He knew the rain fell on the just and the unjust alike. But that didn't mean he was willing to subject himself to the stares and whispers that had been his lot since being released from the hospital three years ago. He was grateful *Gott* had let him buy this farm so he could do everything possible never to leave it. He was able to raise his own fruits and vegetables, grain, meat, eggs and dairy. He could harvest his own firewood. He could, conceivably, leave his property but a few times a year and be absolutely fine. He had his books and his animals.

For the first time in a long time, he realized he missed the human interaction he'd shunned since the accident. Miriam's daily presence made him realize that simple conversation wasn't something to dread but enjoy. And his neighbors, the Kemps… Well, when little Hannah had stared at him that morning, he'd braced himself for fear or an unpleasant comment from the child. Instead, she had offered to let him see her doll. To Aaron, that simple moment was a marvelous thing.

Yes, if he hadn't broken his arm and come to rely on Miriam to get him through his daily chores, he never would have known what he was missing. He didn't know whether to bless or curse her for that.

Chapter Seven

On Monday morning, Miriam walked over to Aaron's to do the morning chores. She hadn't slept well because she'd been wrestling all night with her promise to *Gott* versus the bishop's urging her to revive her midwifery career here in Montana. She was certain there were dark circles under her eyes, and she felt lethargic.

On the farm, she quietly let herself into the back door to fetch the sterilized metal buckets and the clean milk can from the kitchen. Major padded up to her and greeted her with his lumbering enthusiasm, but the house was otherwise quiet. It seemed Aaron was sleeping late.

In the barn, she got right to work. The cows knew her now, and obediently went into the milking stall without complaint. Miriam's hands were now accustomed to the labor required to hand-milk six cows each morning, but she wondered how fast Aaron would recapture his ability to perform the same task once the cast was off his arm. She had a feeling she would be milking for a week or two extra…

"Miriam?"

She whirled around. Emma stood in the barn doorway, her hand resting on her pregnant belly. Miriam jerked upright off the milking stool. "Emma! Are you okay? Is the baby okay?"

"*Ja*, I'm fine, but a man from church brought his son to our house looking for you. He has a cut and wonders if you can take a look at it."

Miriam looked at the unfinished milking ahead of her and made a fast decision. "*Ja*, sure. I'll milk the rest of the cows after I take a look."

"I'll let them know you'll be right over."

Miriam released the half-milked cow over to her calf, who immediately dove in for an extra-rich breakfast. Miriam smiled at the tableau, then hastily followed her sister-in-law back to the Kemp farm. A horse and buggy rested in the driveway.

A man who looked to be in his early forties stood in Emma's kitchen while a young boy sat at the kitchen table with a bloody towel over his forearm. Little Hannah watched, wide-eyed.

"Miriam, this is Moses King and his son, Amos," Emma introduced quickly.

"*Guder mariye*," the man said. "Amos, he cut his arm on a piece of glass. Can you look?"

"*Ja*, of course." Miriam snatched up another kitchen chair and sat down, then gently took the boy's arm in her lap. "Let's see what you did here, Amos," she said, in what she called her *soothing nurse's voice*.

Unflinching, the boy allowed her to peel back the bloody towel. A three-inch gash on the underside of his arm oozed fresh blood as she did so. She peered at the cut. As dramatic as it was, she was fairly certain the glass had not cut any tendons or nerves, which was her biggest concern.

"Can you move your fingers?" she asked the boy. "Like this?" And she wiggled her fingers.

"*Ja*," he replied, and waggled his fingers. The action brought a fresh oozing to the wound, but Miriam was vastly relieved. No permanent injury.

She looked at Moses. "It looks like a good clean cut with no lasting damage. I'm going to wash him up and apply some stitches, but he'll need a tetanus shot—something I can't do here. You'll have to take him to the clinic in town."

"*Ja, gut*," he replied. "Please, do what you can."

Miriam folded the towel back over the wound and asked the boy, "Can you wait here for a couple of minutes? I'll need to fetch some supplies."

The child nodded. Miriam placed his arm on the table and dashed outside and toward her cabin. She had a goodly amount of medical supplies stashed in a trunk, so she yanked open the chest and rummaged until she found what she needed.

Back in Emma's kitchen, the boy had not moved, and she blessed his stoic temperament. "Okay, let's get you cleaned up," she told him. "You're a brave young man."

The child gave her a tremulous smile as she peeled back the towel once more. Then a thought occurred to her, and she looked at the boy's father. "Moses, can you do me a favor? I was in the middle of milking Aaron's cows when Emma fetched me, and I wasn't finished. Can you go to Aaron's and explain the situation? Tell him I'll be back as soon as I can to finish up."

"*Ja*, of course." Moses touched his son's head, then turned and walked out of the kitchen.

"Now, let's get you fixed up." Miriam smiled at the boy. "After I clean away the mess, I'm going to put a medicine called lidocaine on your skin before I stitch you up. It will make part of your arm go numb. You won't feel a thing when I put in the stitches—I promise. Can you continue to be brave?"

"*Ja*," said the child with a slight tremor.

She donned thin latex gloves. It took just a few minutes to wipe away the blood with an antiseptic. Then Miriam applied some lidocaine to the wound. "What that ointment is doing is making your skin go to sleep. Then I'll pretend I'm sewing a quilt on your arm!" She grinned at the boy and was rewarded with a smile back.

Within a few minutes, she'd prepared to suture the wound. "*Ach*, you'll be right as rain when I'm finished," she told him.

Just then, Moses reentered the house. "Aaron said it was fine, take as long as you need," he told her.

"I won't be much longer. Your son is remarkably brave, Moses. I haven't had such a *gut* patient in a long time."

He beamed at his son and peered over Miriam's shoulder to watch the process. The room was silent as she neatly stitched up the wound. "These will have to stay in for about ten days," she told the boy. "You'll have to do your best not to get it dirty." She looked at Moses. "Do you have some over-the-counter pain medicine at home? Acetaminophen or ibuprofen?"

"Ja."

"Then make sure he gets what he needs to control

any pain after the topical anesthetic wears off." She finished the last stitch. "There! What do you think, Amos? Did I make a nice quilt?"

The boy smiled and scrutinized his arm. "Looks *gut*," he proclaimed. "Can I show my friends?"

"Well, it's going to have to stay covered for a little while." Miriam applied a generous amount of antibiotic ointment to a piece of gauze, which she placed over the wound. Then she grabbed two colors of elastic adhesive-wrap tape. "Which color do you want—blue or green?"

"Green, *bitte*," he replied.

"Green it is." She wrapped his arm. "Now, make sure you don't get it wet for a couple of days, *ja*?"

"*Ja*," he replied. As Miriam released his arm, he experimentally touched the bandage. "It doesn't hurt as bad as I thought it would. *Danke*."

"*Ja, vielen dank*," Moses chimed in with heartfelt emotion.

"*Bitte*," she replied. "But I'm serious about getting him a tetanus shot. Trust me, you don't want him getting tetanus."

"I will. What do you say, Amos?" Moses asked his son. "Shall we go into town right now? Afterward, I can get you an ice-cream cone."

"Ja!" The boy hopped out of the chair. "Can it be chocolate?"

"Of course." He winked at Miriam, who chuckled and started gathering her supplies.

After father and son had departed, Emma dropped into a kitchen chair. "That was well done," she said simply. "You're talented."

"Danke." Miriam shrugged. "I'm just glad I have a

stock of medical supplies I brought with me. The cut was clean, so it was no problem to sew him up." She glanced at the clock. "Can I leave my supplies here and pick them up after I'm finished at Aaron's? I feel bad leaving him in the lurch."

"*Ja*, of course. Meanwhile, I'll wash this towel." Emma picked up the forgotten bloody cloth with a thumb and forefinger. "I'll return it to Moses later on."

Miriam hurried down the driveway and across the road. Despite the interrupted morning, she had to admit it felt good to help little Amos King. And because it felt good, she felt guilty.

She reentered the barn and saw Aaron, who was sitting on the milking stool in front of a cow, fiddling with something. "What news?" he asked as she approached.

"It's fine. Amos King had quite a gash on his arm. I sewed him up and suggested his dad take him to the clinic for a tetanus shot."

"That's *gut*, then." He leveled a look at her. "Seems a shame to leave those skills behind."

Miriam turned away. He was right. She knew she was skilled. Her determination to get the medical training she wanted, even at the expense of leaving the church, was nothing short of a calling. It's why it was the only gift she could think of to offer *Gott* in exchange for forgiveness.

But none of this was something she felt like explaining. "I can finish the milking now," she said, as a means of distraction.

"Okay." He got off the milking stool.

Miriam grabbed one of the metal buckets, put it under the cow's udder, buried her forehead in the animal's flank and got to work. The warm, sweet-smelling milk zinged into the bucket.

Not for anything would she admit the feeling of satisfaction she'd experienced after sewing up Amos's wound. She hoped *Gott* wasn't angry with her for using her medical skills after promising Him to give them up.

While Miriam finished milking, Aaron squatted down next to Polly, a cow who had already been milked. He was still experimenting with a one-handed milking device and trying to figure out the details.

"I'm finished," Miriam announced, pouring the last of the milk into the milk can and then putting on the lid.

"*Gut.* Can you help me with this?" He held out a rubber cup to her.

"*Ja*, sure. What is this?" Miriam took the item and regarded it questioningly.

"It's the prototype for the one-handed milker I'm designing," he explained. "I'm still working things out. Can you try inverting the ends of the cup like this?" He demonstrated as best he could.

Miriam tucked the rubber end inward. "Like this?"

"*Ja.* Now, let me see if this works." He squatted down beside the patient cow and slipped the cup over one of the quarters. "That's an improvement."

Miriam leaned over, watching him. "I'm afraid I still don't quite grasp how this is supposed to work," she remarked.

He stood up and explained as best he could. "When we milk a cow, we squeeze the milk out. But when a calf nurses, it draws the milk out by creating suction with its mouth." He gestured toward Polly's calf. "I'm thinking if I can make a device that creates suction, it should do the same thing—draw the milk out. So if I fit a stiff rubber cup over like this—" he demonstrated once more "—with a short hose leading into a jar or container, then a small hand pump will draw out the milk and direct it into a jar. If it works the way I'm thinking, then it can all be done with one hand. For someone with arthritis, it means they don't have to keep squeezing while milking their animal. This milks it for them."

Miriam stared at it for a moment or two, her eyebrows drawn together in concentration. Then her expression cleared. "I think I get it! Aaron, that's brilliant!"

The feeling of pleasure that washed through him at her praise was sweet. "I just hope it works," he said modestly.

She gave him a smile that weakened his knees. "You *do* have an inventive mind," she said. "Never in a million years would I have thought of this. What else have you made?"

He shrugged. "Just a few items to make things easier around a farm."

"Show me."

He glanced at her. She seemed genuinely interested. "You haven't seen my workshop, have you?"

She shook her head. *"Nein."*

"Then I suppose that's the first place to go. But let's get the milk into the house first."

Miriam loaded the milk can onto the hand truck, strapped it on and trundled the heavy item toward the house. Aaron followed with the empty metal buckets. With his one good hand, he helped her bring the can into the kitchen. Then, with Major's enormous black shape lumbering beside them, he walked her to the shed adjacent to the garden, where he did most of his experimentation.

"Wow," she breathed, stepping inside.

The shed was neatly laid out with the various tools he used to work wood and metal. An L-shaped workbench dominated most of the space, and a variety of tools hung from the walls on nails and hooks. Most of the work shed was, by his standards, pretty ordinary. But there was something about the layout that got his creative juices flowing, and often he would tinker until a vague idea became a concrete notion.

"This is one of the things I've worked on," he said, picking up a small angled block of wood with a metal plate screwed over it. "This allows me to sharpen a chisel. Watch." He placed a chisel between the metal plate and the angled wood, then demonstrated how the device allowed more precise and uniform sharpening using sandpaper.

"And this." He pointed to a wheel hoe. "I didn't come up with it, but I made some improvements to an existing design. I make a lot of these for people in the church. Women especially find it's easier to till a kitchen garden with this wheel hoe than try to fit a horse and plow into a garden space."

Then he pointed to a wide PVC pipe with a Y fitting near the base. "This is a chicken feeder that's designed to minimize wasting feed. It also keeps mice out. The top unscrews so grain can be poured in, and chickens eat from the opening of the Y. Most of our church members are using these now."

He touched another item. "This is a lever-arm cheese

press. They're easy to make and a lot cheaper than commercial cheese presses. I saw a plan for these and modified it until I was satisfied. I've made a lot of these— What?" he asked, when he saw the bewildered look on her face.

She dropped onto a high work stool. "Aaron, I had no idea you did all this. This is amazing. You have an unbelievable mind. Have you ever thought about going into manufacturing? I have a feeling lots of people would be interested in these products."

"No."

"But—"

"No. Absolutely not."

"But—"

"Miriam, I said *no*." He felt his temper rise.

She glanced at the ground, then back up at him. "So you won't develop what is an obvious talent—a gift—to make things easier for people. Why not?"

He stared at her. Was she really that dim? "Because it would mean leaving the farm. And I don't want to leave the farm—ever."

"Why not?"

He turned away, shocked at her denseness. "Isn't it obvious?"

"You mean because of your face?"

"*Ja.* What else?" He shot her a dirty look over his shoulder. "I'm hideous. Deformed."

"Don't forget bitter."

He whirled around to face her. "And why shouldn't I be? Over and over again, I've seen how people avoid me, stare at me. The less I have to do with people, the better."

"But you go to church."

"*Ja*, and then I come home. I won't abandon *Gott*,

though sometimes I wonder if He's abandoned me." He caught his breath. That was a little too close to the truth.

"Oh, Aaron..." Miriam's expression was sympathetic. "*Gott* never abandons anyone."

"That's easy to say when you're beautiful. You don't have a face that frightens people."

"It doesn't frighten *me*."

Startled, he jerked his head up. She was looking at him with an enigmatic half smile, a small gleam in her eyes. She truly *was* beautiful. She was also right.

"*Nein*," he said slowly. "I don't frighten you. Why is that?"

"Aaron, I've spent my whole nursing career working around people whose bodies are broken in some way. You're just one of many. You aren't special. You're still *you* underneath your scarred face. Can't you see that?"

"Nein." He fiddled with the chisel sharpener on the workbench. "I can't. And neither can anyone else. That's the problem."

"So you intend to hide yourself away for the rest of your life?"

"Of course. What choice do I have? It's why I've worked so hard to become as self-sufficient as possible. So I don't have to leave the farm or see anyone except on my own terms."

She sighed. "That's not healthy, Aaron."

"I didn't ask for your approval." He heard the hardness in his voice. "I'm just coping as best I can."

"We'll see about that..." she muttered, then said more loudly, "I think I'm ready to learn how to make cheese now. Will you show me how?"

"Nein." The last thing he wanted at the moment was

company. He was too busy wallowing in his all-too-familiar self-pity. Self-pity was easier. It was safer. "Not today, I think."

She looked startled. "But all that milk…"

"I'll take care of it."

"But how can you—"

"I said, I'll take care of it!" he shouted.

To his astonishment, he saw tears spring to her eyes. "Fine." She jumped off the stool. "Suit yourself." She abruptly left the workshop. He watched as her stiff figure disappeared down the driveway.

Aaron slumped down on the high work stool she had just vacated and covered his face with his one good hand. He *was* a monster, and not just because of the scars. Miriam was the first person in years to treat him like a normal human being, and what did he do? Pick a fight and chase her off.

He wondered if she would even come back that afternoon for the barn chores. He certainly wouldn't blame her if she left him to his own devices—it was certainly what he deserved.

He desperately wanted Miriam to stay. What must he do to keep her around? He prayed.

Chapter Eight

"I just don't get it, I guess." Clutching a hot mug of tea in her hands, Miriam sat at the kitchen table and talked with her sympathetic sister-in-law. Little Hannah was out on a playdate, and the house was otherwise quiet.

"He's been a loner as long as we've known him," confirmed Emma. She sipped from her own tea. "He's always been difficult, but all of us in the church community try to be understanding."

"I mean, I've worked with a lot of people who were traumatized over a disfiguring medical condition," continued Miriam. "It takes a long time to adapt, to understand it can't be changed, to accept the truth. But I don't think I've ever met someone so reluctant to face reality. It's been three years. Do you know he's completely set up his farm to be so self-sufficient that he never has to leave it? He even has some women from church collect the things he has for sale, such as milk and cheese and butter, and bring it to town for him."

"*Ja*, that would be Nell Peachey..."

"He also has someone come by to collect any surplus garden produce he has and bring it to town to sell."

"At the Yoders' store..."

"It makes me mad to see him waste his potential. I'm surprised he deigns to come to church." Miriam knew she was working herself into a tizzy, but she didn't care. It felt good to vent to Emma. "He says the only reason he goes is because he can't abandon *Gott*, even if *Gott* abandoned him. Isn't that the most arrogant thing you've ever heard?"

"Well, at least he *does* come to church." Emma smiled. "And he helps with community building projects when asked. Building barns, houses, whatever. He's a *gut* carpenter. Despite his solitary nature, he tries his best."

"Well, I think he's nurtured his martyrdom just a little too much." Miriam glared at a perfectly innocent potted plant in the middle of the table. "To be honest, I was livid yesterday when he told Thomas he'd walk home alone and just left the church potluck after services. It was just plain rude."

"Thomas wasn't offended, if that's any consolation," remarked Emma. "I guess we're just used to his abrupt ways by now."

"Yeah, but he has no reason to be rude to people—*especially* church members who are doing what they can to make him feel welcome."

"Miriam..." Emma's quiet voice pierced Miriam's tirade. "Forgive me for asking, but does your anger stem from purely professional reasons?"

Miriam paused and stared at her sister-in-law. "What do you mean?"

"I mean, as a nurse, you have a long history of dealing with people who are coping with illnesses and injuries in a variety of ways. Why does Aaron's way of coping bother you so much?"

"I guess I hate seeing someone ruining his own life when he could be doing something about it," Miriam hedged. "It's not healthy to let anything fester and become infected. His body has healed from the damage he sustained in the fire, but his mind hasn't. His mind is still infected, so to speak. Rampant infection can kill someone. If Aaron isn't careful, it might kill him."

"Is that all?"

She glared at the other woman. "Isn't that enough?"

"What I mean is, you seem to care for him more than just a professional responsibility to keep his farm running until his broken arm heals."

Miriam drew her eyebrows together. "I don't follow."

"Then I'll be blunt. It seems you're developing some personal feelings for Aaron. Or am I wrong?"

Miriam was honestly thunderstruck. In the sudden silence, she heard the ticking of the kitchen clock.

Was she developing personal feelings for Aaron? Is that why his stubborn reluctance to release the grief over his accident three years ago bothered her on such a profound level?

"I—I don't know," she finally said, faltering. "I never thought about it."

"Well, regardless, I think you're the best thing that's happened to Aaron in a long time—probably since his accident." Emma dipped her tea bag in and out of her mug. "For the first time, he's being forced to interact with someone, whether he likes it or not. To be honest, I'm surprised he accepted a ride to church with us in the first place. That's a first for him. So maybe, at last, he's taking baby steps toward a recovery. Not a physical recovery, as you pointed out, but a mental one."

"And you think I'm responsible?"

"*Ja*, of course. The rest of us haven't had any luck with him. It's only you who's been interacting with him on a regular basis."

"Until he chases me off." Miriam scowled at her mug.

"But, as you've pointed out, that's his way of coping. A wounded animal lashes out when it's in pain. His arm or his face may not be painful anymore, but he still has emotional pain. And that means you, dear sister-in-law, are in a unique position to help him."

"But how?" She slumped lower in her chair. "He rebuffs every effort."

"By persistence. Miriam, you're a nurse. You should know that better than anyone."

"I suppose..."

"And the fact that you're taking his snarly attitude personally is what makes me think your interest in him is transitioning from professional into something more."

Miriam shook her head. "*Nein*, I don't think so, Emma."

The clock in the kitchen chimed softly. Emma glanced at it, then rose to her feet. "I have to go get Hannah from her playdate. Do you want to come with me?"

"*Nein*, I think I'll go rest in my cabin for a bit." Miriam sighed. "Thanks for letting me vent, Emma."

Emma nodded. "Something to keep in mind when dealing with Aaron too. Maybe he just needs an opportunity to vent. I don't know if he's ever had that chance."

Miriam returned to her little guest house in a thoughtful mood. It was embarrassing to think Emma may have pegged her more closely than even she—Miriam—was willing to admit.

Was she developing feelings for Aaron?

The rare times she'd seen him smile, she'd been astounded at how it transformed his face. His eyes crinkled, and the scars were less noticeable; he was quite a breathtakingly handsome man underneath the disfigurement. She wondered why he hadn't gotten married, before the accident.

It was then she realized she knew very little about his past. He'd never volunteered information about his family or his home back in Pennsylvania. She certainly knew nothing about the accident that had changed his life, except what little information his fellow church members knew.

Absently, she brewed herself another cup of tea and sat down in the rocking chair on the tiny porch, looking out at the peaceful fields around the farm, with the high peaks of the Bitterroot Mountains visible over the tops of the trees.

Underneath the growly exterior, there was a core of kindness within Aaron; it was evident in how he treated his animals—and more, how his animals responded to him. His dog, Major, loved him profoundly. So did his cats. His cows were affectionate with him. So were the horses. Even his chickens allowed him to pet them. Aaron's relationship with his pets and his livestock indicated one of two things: either he was so achingly lonely for human company that he transferred his affections to animals—or deep down, he was just a kind man.

She suspected it was both.

She thought about what he'd said a short time ago: *"That's easy to say when you're beautiful. You don't have a face that frightens people."*

Beautiful. Did Aaron think she was beautiful? Miriam honestly hadn't given her looks much thought one way or another. She had always considered herself fairly ordinary. But evidently, Aaron didn't feel the same way.

For a brief moment, she worried that Aaron might be romantically fixating on her simply because she was the first woman he'd been in close contact with on a daily basis, presumably since his accident.

But the worry instantly receded when she realized she didn't mind. If she was honest with herself, she wanted to get to know Aaron better. Get to know what his background was; what the circumstances surrounding his accident were; and what had made him turn his back on his friends, family and church in Pennsylvania and launch himself all the way across the country to Montana.

In short, there was a lot about him she didn't know… but she wanted to.

If he would let her.

It was like he had locked himself in a box, and she held the key. What kind of treasure would she find inside if she was successful?

She smiled to herself. Aaron had kicked her off his farm for the moment, but she would return in a couple of hours to do the evening chores. Hopefully, he'd have had a chance to cool off. Regardless of whether he wanted her help in making cheese or not, she would dedicate her days to aiding in whatever other tasks needed doing.

Little by little, she would help him emerge from his box. Maybe getting him to vent—to open up some painful wounds and let the infection clear—was the key.

She would be cheerful. She would be patient. She would be understanding. She was a trained nurse, after all, and Aaron was just the last in a long line of patients she had helped heal.

And if he thought she was beautiful…well, she didn't mind at all.

Aaron spent the entire day kicking himself mentally. How could he have treated Miriam the way he had?

Awkwardly, he worked on making two batches of cheddar cheese. His injured arm wasn't hurting much anymore, and he had some use of those fingers, so he was able to pour milk into the pots, add culture and rennet, stir when needed, check the thermometer, and otherwise work on the slow and patient steps necessary to turn liquid milk into solid cheese.

But the lengthy process gave him ample time to think—and inevitably, that led to a great deal of remorse in how he had responded to Miriam. He was like a wounded animal, lashing out in pain. Miriam didn't deserve that.

She was the first person to treat him like a human being in years. Or was she? As she'd pointed out, church members had been treating him as they would any other member of their community. Just yesterday, for example, he had chatted pleasantly with Adam Chupp while in line for food. And he had eaten the meal while seated with Thomas and his family.

And little Hannah—well, he almost wanted to weep when she'd shown him her doll.

He had a decent camaraderie with the men in the church, thanks to the numerous times he had joined them in barn raisings and other construction projects, but he purposely avoided being around women and children. He dreaded seeing anyone turning aside or avoiding him. Or worse, being stared at.

Then Hannah had offered to show him her doll. That little moment remained burned in his mind. The small act had made him feel…well, human. Ordinary.

Was he making too big a deal about his scars? Doubtless, that's what Miriam would say—but then, she wasn't the one living with them.

He took a long knife and cut the curds in one of the pots of cheese, then set a small kitchen timer to let the curds rest for five minutes. After that, he gently began increasing the heat under the pot. Making cheddar cheese was mostly a matter of following the right steps, maintaining the right temperature for the right amount of time and being patient.

Would Miriam come tonight to do the barn chores? Or had he chased her off permanently?

He glanced at the kitchen table and wondered if she would notice there were now two chairs, not just one. The other chair had been stored in the barn. This afternoon, he had brought it back in the house and dusted it off. After all, there might be an instance when both he and Miriam might want to sit down at the same time.

Thinking about Miriam led to thoughts of courtship. He might be reading too much into her acceptance of his appearance, but she was a woman who didn't recoil from him and treated him just the same as any other man. Would she ever welcome his attentions?

He gripped the long-handled wooden spoon he used to stir the pots on the stove. *Nein.* He wouldn't try to court her. Just the thought of another rejection made his gut clench. He didn't want to put Miriam in the position of having to turn him down.

He looked out the kitchen window at the beautiful farm he had created single-handedly since arriving in Montana. *Gott* had provided him the means to make a *gut* living while seeing as few people as possible. But did *He* mean for him to live the rest his whole life alone? The years stretched ahead of him, bleak and lonely. Ten years from now, he would be doing the same thing—stirring cheese on a stove while looking out a window. Twenty years from now, thirty years from now…

A movement out the window suddenly caught his eye.

It was Miriam, walking up the driveway. As was typical in the evening, she bypassed the house and went straight to the barn to feed the cows, attend to the chickens and call the animals in for the night.

She had come back. He hadn't frightened her off permanently with his bad temper after all.

He grinned and turned his attention back to the cheese. It was at a critical moment, and he couldn't leave it alone. But he knew—or at least, he hoped—Miriam would come into the house afterward, as was her habit.

He stirred and monitored the cheese, his ears straining to hear her footsteps outside, his heart beating faster than normal. Would she simply do the barn chores out of a sense of duty? Or would she come into the house and allow him to apologize?

At long last, he heard the crunch of feet on gravel. Then came her voice, talking to the dog. She didn't sound cross or angry. He took a deep breath. "*Danke*, *Gott*," he whispered.

"Aaron?" Miriam opened the kitchen door. "I just finished the barn chores."

Her voice sounded normal. Aaron felt his tightened midsection relax a bit. *"Guder nammidaag."* He turned to face her. "I owe you a huge apology, Miriam. I had no right to bite your head off this morning, and I'm sorry for it."

She gave him a bright smile that weakened his knees. "You're a tough nut to crack, Aaron, but I'm trying my best."

"Trying your best to do what?"

"To draw you out of your shell. It's about time, don't you think?"

"But I don't want to be drawn out. I'm fine the way I am."

"If you say so." She seemed unperturbed. But then she noticed the second chair at the table. "Aaron, I didn't know you had two chairs."

"The other one was in the barn. I thought it might be needed, now that you're working here."

But she merely nodded. "An extra chair is always needed. I see you're managing to make cheese one-handed. Want some help?"

"*Ja*, sure." It wasn't just the extra hands that would be welcome—he didn't want her to leave again. "I'm about ready to put the curds into the press. Two hands are better than one and a half."

She followed his instructions to line the cheese press with a clean, sterile cloth; then she poured the curds into it and settled the weights in place.

He made a deliberate effort to be pleasant, and to his surprise, within a few minutes, they were chatting about various matters—the news, a bit of church gossip and what was happening in town.

Part of him was astonished. Was this all there was to it? Was it just a matter of…well, being nice?

"You said you cure this in a root cellar?" Miriam asked when the tasks were completed.

"*Ja.* They need a cool, humid environment."

"Where's your root cellar?"

"Out back. I guess I never showed it to you, did I?" He risked a smile. "Perhaps it's *hochmut* to admit, but it's actually rather a neat place. *Komm*, I'll show you. But first, let me light a lantern."

He touched a match to a kerosene hurricane lantern and led her outside toward a mound with a set of steps leading down to a half-underground enclosure. When he opened the door and showed her inside, she paused. "Wow," she breathed. "Aaron, this is amazing."

He smiled again. Smiling was becoming easier for him. Almost. "*Danke.* It took a lot of work, but it's part of how I earn my living."

The cinder block–sided room had a gravel floor and lots of wooden shelves. Each shelf had wire racks to prop the cheese an inch above the wood and allow air to circulate on all sides. The shelves also had dates written on tape so he could track their aging process. At the back of the root cellar was a heavy curtain, behind which he stored garden produce.

"'Cheddar,' 'Swiss,' 'Parmesan,'" she read out loud. "And you said you also make mozzarella and cream cheese?"

"*Ja*, but those are fresh and don't need aging."

Miriam shook her head. "Aaron, I don't think I've ever met anyone as clever and resourceful as you."

In the wavering lamplight, her eyes were nearly black and her face shadowed, but he saw something then that he never, ever thought he'd see in a woman's face again: admiration, respect and maybe—just maybe—affection. Or was he imagining things?

Either way, it scared him. The root cellar suddenly seemed too close, too intimate. He backed up a step or two. "*Danke.* Uh, I guess it's getting late. I'm sure you'll want to go home."

"*Ja*, it's getting late." She smiled, almost as if she could read his mind. It was a profoundly disquieting thought. The last thing he wanted was to bare his emotions and vulnerabilities.

She turned and preceded him out the door and up the steps. He followed, blowing out the lantern in the evening sunlight.

"I'll see you tomorrow morning," she said, smiling again. Then, without another word, she walked away.

To Aaron, it almost seemed as if she took the evening light with her.

Chapter Nine

Miriam laid her plans before her brother and sister-in-law while they were all eating breakfast the next morning. "I've decided I'm going to try to draw Aaron out of his shell," she remarked. "He seems more willing to be drawn out. Any ideas how I can help him?"

"We've been remiss," said Thomas. "Here we are, his closest neighbors, yet we've never done much by way of including him in events or gatherings. He does the bare minimum with the community and then goes home."

"Barn or house-raisings are always large events," commented Miriam. "Places he can just get lost in the crowd. I don't think he likes going to them, but he also recognizes he can't necessarily avoid everything and still remain a member of the church. But it's the one-on-one interactions that I think make him uneasy. Personally, I believe he's been solitary for so long, he's just out of practice."

"Would he accept an invitation to dinner, do you suppose?" Emma rested one hand on her widening midsection. "I mean, we're probably the people he's most familiar with. It might be a *gut* way to get him more comfortable being around people again."

"*Ja*, sure!" Miriam grinned at her sister-in-law.

"Absolutely!" confirmed Thomas. He blew a kiss at his wife. "*Gut* idea!"

Hannah banged her spoon on her plate. "I'll make cookies!"

Miriam was surprised her young niece was following the conversation so well. "What kind?" she teased the child.

"Chocolate chip."

"As if I didn't know." Miriam chuckled, then addressed Emma. "What day do you want to invite him over?"

"This evening would work. Would that work for you, *lieb*?" Emma asked Thomas.

"*Ja*. I'm working in the home office today rather than at the store, so that's fine. I'll be done early."

"I'll ask him, then," she Miriam. "I can go do his barn chores this morning, then come back and help with dinner. Do you have anything in mind?"

"I could make quiche." Emma's eyes twinkled. "Since I know it's your favorite. We have plenty of broccoli and onions in the garden—and of course, lots of eggs."

"Well, you won't find me arguing against *that*." Miriam grinned.

"Go on, then. Go ask if he'll come." Emma rose from the table. "In fact, I'll make more than enough, and he can take extra home with him."

Miriam deposited her dishes in the sink, grabbed her work gloves and kissed her niece goodbye. "Say a prayer he accepts," she called out to her brother and sister-in-law as she left.

Walking the short distance between her brother's home and Aaron's farm, she said a prayer of her own. Aaron *did* seem as if he were slowly loosening up. She prayed she was doing the right thing. But would he refuse the invitation?

Though she was bursting with eagerness to ask him, Miriam deliberately kept to her usual routine. Milking the cows took an hour, and then she needed to clean the stalls, make sure the chickens had fresh water, attend to the barn cats, and make sure everything was clean and orderly. Then she loaded the milk can onto the hand truck and wheeled it to the back door of the house.

Aaron was already in the kitchen, removing the cheese from their presses. *"Guder mariye."* He smiled at her.

"*Guder mariye*," she replied. Already, the day seemed better. She realized how much she enjoyed seeing his rare smiles. It was always like a little ray of sunshine had burst over his head and illuminated his face. "I have a question for you—Do you like quiche?"

"*Ja*, sure. Who doesn't? I seldom have it, though." He lifted the weight from the press and put it to one side.

"My sister-in-law makes an absolutely mouthwatering quiche. She uses your Swiss cheese, in fact, and she packs it with bacon and broccoli and onions." Miriam dragged the large, heavy can toward the sink and prepared to strain the milk.

"Stop," he joked. "You're making me hungry."

"That's what I was hoping. Thomas and Emma want to know if you'd like to come to dinner tonight. Emma said she would make quiche—and in fact, she said she'd make enough to send some home with you."

He froze. "Uh… Uh, n-n-no…" he stuttered.

Dipping some milk through the straining cloth, she continued. "You've never seen the little cottage Thomas built me. It's a beauty, Aaron—and as someone with your carpentry skills, you'll appreciate it."

"Um…"

"You should see all the pretty little personal touches Emma added too." Miriam soldiered on, hoping to distract him with details. "She figured out quick enough that my favorite soap she makes is lemon, so I get to use that all day long. You should let her know your favorite, too, Aaron. She'd be happy to make some specially for you."

"Uh…no. I—I can't go."

She saw the panicked look in his eyes and met them squarely. "Why not?"

He scowled. "You know why…"

"Oh, come on, Aaron. Thomas and Emma know what you look like. Why deprive them of the pleasure of your company for dinner?"

"I'd rather not."

"You're becoming a hermit."

"Of course. Isn't it obvious?"

Miriam continued straining the milk. She filled one jar, put it aside and then grabbed another. Then she dipped more milk out of the can. "You know, Aaron, there comes a point where your inclination to be alone isn't much more than a painful wound. I've seen that enough during my nursing career. Wounds that fester don't heal."

"I'm healed." His words were short. "I'm about as healed as I'll ever be."

"Oh, sure, on the outside. But not on the inside. That's what's painful."

He stared at the floor and said nothing.

"Besides," she continued, "it would be rude to refuse, especially when my sister-in-law is going to make a delicious dinner."

"It's not rude." If anything, he scowled harder. "It's just…just…"

"Just rude, is what it is." Miriam decided to change tactics. "Please, Aaron. It would mean a lot to them. They're such nice people, and they'd really like to be neighborly."

Finally, she saw him wavering.

"And it would mean a lot to me too," she added softly.

She saw his eyes widen, then soften. He heaved a martyred sigh. "*Oll recht*, I'll come. What time?"

"I'll come by for the evening chores, and then we can both go over together. How does that sound?"

"Fine." There was a sense of doom in his voice.

She had to resist the urge to lean over and kiss him on the cheek. "You're just a little out of practice with making conversation, that's all," she said. "But all you have to do is ask Emma about her soaps or her garden, or ask Thomas about his bookkeeping business, and they'll do all the talking. All you have to do is listen and look interested."

She was rewarded with a small, strained smile. "*Ja*, sure," he said weakly.

"*Gut*, then." She'd finished straining the milk, so she capped the jars and placed them in the icebox for cooling. "Should I make butter today? It looks like there's enough cream."

"*Ja.* And Nell Peachey is coming today to collect some cheese to bring to town to sell." He passed a hand over his face as if to wipe away the dread of the dinner invitation.

Miriam hoped the plan wouldn't backfire and result in Aaron shutting himself away even more once the dinner was over. But she couldn't imagine better people to help Aaron than her brother and sister-in-law. Nor did she know what else to do to help him ease the emotional pain from his injury. "I'll get started on butter, then."

She pulled yesterday's milk out and began ladling the cream into a pot to warm up. There were also a couple of gallons of cream already in jars, which she poured into the pot as well.

Meanwhile, working with diminished efficiency, Aaron managed to get the cheese unwrapped from the cheesecloth and placed the unripe cheese on a rack. His face was drawn and grim.

She decided to relent. "Aaron, did I push too far? Would you truly rather not come to dinner tonight?"

He paused, sighing. "*Nein*, I'll come. I think you're right—the longer I stay by myself, the more it's not healthy. And I like your brother and sister-in-law. They've been *gut* neighbors."

Relief washed over her. She realized just how much she wanted Aaron to recover. Finally, she gave in to the impulse and kissed him on the cheek, which just happened to be the scarred side. "*Danke*, Aaron. It will mean a lot to them." She turned back to the pot of cream, which she heaved onto the stove. She clipped a thermometer onto the side of the pot, switched on the propane and went to find a long-handled spoon.

She found Aaron frozen, staring at her, his face red. "Are you *oll recht*?" she inquired.

He snapped awake. "*Ja*, sure. Uh, I need to go get some cheese from the root cellar for when Nell arrives. Be right back." He practically ran out of the kitchen.

She watched him descend the small flight of steps and open the root cellar door, then disappear inside. What was all that about? She shrugged and turned to stir the cream on the stove.

And she prayed Aaron was at last on the road to recovery.

Aaron fled into the quiet of the semi-subterranean root cellar and paused, hand to his chest, breathing hard. The darkness of the damp space offered a welcome respite.

She'd kissed him. She'd actually kissed his scarred face. He knew he was overreacting to what was merely a casual gesture, but still…she'd *kissed* him.

He strove to regain his composure. Miriam's spontaneous action merely confirmed what he already suspected: he was falling hopelessly in love with her. But it was obviously one-sided.

If such a simple and friendly gesture could throw him into such a tizzy, then she was right about him. But one thing was certain: he was determined to keep his feelings under wraps. He had come to value not just Miriam's assistance on the farm but also her friendship. No, *value* wasn't the right word. It was deeper than that; he had come to *cherish* her.

For that reason, he vowed to keep his feelings to himself. The last thing he wanted to do was chase her away because she didn't—or couldn't—return the sentiment.

Thus armed, he fumbled around in the darkness where he knew the ripened Swiss cheese was stacked and selected two rounds before reemerging from the root cellar. He needed a crate to hold the cheese Nell stopped by to collect, something he clearly hadn't thought to bring with him on his panicked flight from the kitchen, but this Swiss was for Emma Kemp as a thank-you for the dinner invitation.

Composed, he returned to the kitchen to find Miriam engaged in turning the handle of the butter churn.

"I thought Emma might like these blocks of Swiss," he said as he held out the cheese, glad to note his voice sounded normal. "She can use them for the quiche."

"Ach, *danke*. She says you make the best Swiss she's ever tasted." Miriam eyed him. "Are you all right?"

"*Ja*, fine. But I realized I'll need a crate to get all the cheese Nell will be taking, and I might need an extra hand to carry it out of the root cellar." He raised his cast and hoped the excuse for abruptly fleeing the kitchen sounded legitimate.

"Do you need me right away, or can I finish churning the butter first?"

"*Nein*, I won't need you right away. I'll go get the crate and pack it, and by the time I'm done, the butter should be finished."

Pleased with how normal he had managed to make the exchange, he collected the hurricane lamp and a crate, then went back into the cellar. He lit the lamp and started packing the crate.

When Miriam had finished with the butter, she

helped him carry the crate of cheese from the root cellar, then picked up the two blocks of Swiss cheese. "I'm off to help Emma make quiche," she told him. "I'll be back in a few hours. I'll do the evening chores early so we can go back for dinner. Does that sound *gut*?"

"*Ja, danke*. And, uh, Miriam…tell Emma and Thomas *danke* for the invitation."

She smiled and departed. The intermission allowed him to prepare himself for something he hadn't experienced in years: a family dinner. If he had to go through with it, he was glad the invitation came from the Kemps. Miriam was right: it wasn't like they didn't know what he looked like. And they had always been fine neighbors.

He went about doing what chores he could do with one hand. He lavished some affection on Major. And gradually, as the hours passed, he started really looking forward to dinner.

When Miriam returned for the evening chores, he told her as much.

Her face lit up. "That's *gut*, then. Emma is so excited to have you over. She's been fussing and cleaning house and making sure everything's tidy. She has a lot of energy, for a woman whose baby is due in four weeks."

Aaron chuckled. It sounded rusty even to him, but it felt good. "I've done what chores I can, so hopefully there won't be much for you to do. Meanwhile, I'll just go clean up."

Miriam headed for the barn, and Aaron went to change his shirt, comb his hair and make sure his face—such as it was—was clean.

Half an hour later, he and Miriam walked down his

long driveway, crossed the gravel road and made their way toward the Kemp house.

"I haven't been here in a long time," he remarked, looking at the setup critically. "They've done a lot. The garden is beautiful."

"Do you want to see the cabin Thomas built for me?" He heard the excitement in her voice.

"*Ja*, sure."

She led the way, bypassing the house and walking toward the back, where a small building was nestled under a grove of pine and fir trees.

"Oh, it *is* nice." The little building had a welcoming air, with its small front porch and rocking chair.

"Come inside." Miriam opened the door and stood aside to let him enter. "Isn't this just the coziest little house you could imagine?"

Aaron looked around. She was right. The woodwork shone, the late-evening sunshine poured through the western window and he could smell the lemon scent of Emma's famous soap. A floor-to-ceiling bookshelf was stuffed with volumes, and he saw overflow books lodged in various corners. A tiny woodstove—unused, since the weather was warm—was ensconced in a corner. At the back, a curtain revealed a small bedchamber.

"I can see why you like it," he said. "It's small but utterly complete." It embodied a cozy domesticity that his cabin sorely lacked. Miriam had long ago cleaned his home and scolded him for his bachelor standards, but what was missing in his cabin was a woman's touch. Here, it was nothing *but* a woman's touch.

"I almost cried when I saw it," she confessed, smiling as she gazed around the interior. "Thomas did so much work, all for me. And then Emma came in and made curtains and such, and it's just so cozy." Her face shone.

He tried not to stare at Miriam's pure beauty. His plan to keep his feelings for this woman to himself would, he realized, be continually challenged.

"Miriam? Aaron?" Emma's voice called out from the back of the house.

"*Ja*, here we are." Miriam exited the guest house, and Aaron followed. "I was showing Aaron what a beautiful job you and Thomas did on my cabin."

Emma smiled at Aaron. "She loves that cabin," she chuckled. "Aaron, *danke* for the cheese. Are you hungry?"

"*Ja*, actually, I am." Aaron followed Miriam into the main house through the back door.

The house was filled with mouthwatering smells. Aaron looked around the welcoming space. Like Miriam's cottage, it embodied the domestic beauty only a woman could provide. The long room had a kitchen at one side, painted in soothing tones of sage and cream, and a living room on the other, furnished with a braided-rag rug and worn but comfortable furniture. Children's toys and books were in one corner.

"Dinner is almost ready," said Emma, peeking into the oven.

"*Gut'n owed*, Aaron," said Thomas, coming out of one of the bedrooms. He shook Aaron's hand. "Glad you could make it to dinner."

"*Danke* for having me…" Aaron began, before he was interrupted by five-year-old Hannah, who walked up to him with a book in her arms.

"Read me a story?" the child requested.

"*Nein*, *liebling*, he's here for dinner," Thomas admonished gently.

But Aaron was enchanted with the brave and fearless child, who seemed to have no concern whatsoever for his distorted face. "*Ja*, I'll read you a story."

He'd once hoped to one day have children of his own. That hope had long since been dashed, and it seemed no child had willingly approached him since. Hannah's unquestioning acceptance made his eyes well up with tears.

"Just one story, Hannah. Your *mamm* nearly has dinner ready." Thomas shared a wink with Aaron over the precocious child's head.

Aaron sat down in a padded rocking chair, and Hannah climbed into his lap. Aaron's hand shook just a bit as he turned the pages and read about Peter Rabbit's adventures in a garden. He had to resist the urge to hug the child.

Suddenly, a wave of something like jealousy washed over Aaron. Thomas was just a couple years older, but he had a lovely wife, a beautiful stepdaughter and a baby soon to be born. Would he, Aaron, ever have the domestic happiness of the Kemp household? His eyes went to Miriam, busy setting the table as Emma withdrew several quiches from the oven. Her tidy *kapp* and apron over her dark red dress seemed to him to be the height of beauty.

"Hannah, Aaron, *komm* and eat," said Emma as he finished up the story. Aaron lifted Hannah down from his lap, and the girl took his hand to lead him to the table.

When the time came to ask for a blessing over the

food, Aaron found himself praying for *Gott* to bless him with a family. Someday.

Perhaps—just perhaps—he had a future. Maybe he was finally climbing out of the dark abyss he had fallen into after the accident.

If that was the case, he owed it to Miriam. Whether or not he would ever have a chance to court her, he was grateful she had come into his life…even if he'd had to break an arm to find her.

Chapter Ten

Miriam had barely lifted her first taste of quiche to her mouth when she heard the rapid *clip-clop* of horses' hooves going past the house.

"Someone's in a hurry," observed Thomas, taking a bite.

But rather than passing by and fading away, the sound of the hooves got closer. Emma stood up from the table, then Thomas, to peer out the window. A buggy with a panting horse pulled up, and a man catapulted out of the buggy seat.

"It's Daniel Hostetler!" Daniel exclaimed. He strode over to the front door and yanked it open. "Daniel!"

"*Gut'n owed*, Thomas," Daniel said, breathing hard. "Is Miriam here?"

Startled, Miriam stood up. She remembered meeting Daniel briefly after church last Sunday, and she remembered his wife Eva was very pregnant. Her stomach clenched.

"Is Eva in labor?" she guessed.

"*Ja. Bitte*, can you come with me to attend her? She asked for you."

Panic drenched her. She closed her eyes for a moment and saw a young woman having seizures as she tried to give birth…

"I can't," she croaked, opening her eyes and backing up a step. "Daniel, I can't…"

The other man looked bewildered. "But she asked for you," he repeated. "She'd rather not go to the hospital in town, not when a midwife is so close by. And she's in labor right now."

"I can't…" Miriam said once more. What if she lost another mother and baby?

"Miriam." Emma looked stern. "You're the most experienced midwife in the community. Eva needs your help."

Then, surprisingly, Aaron was beside her. He took her by the shoulders and gave her a gentle shake. "Emma's right," he said. "You need to get back on the horse that bucked you. You have all the training in the world, Miriam. *You can do this.*"

Miriam blinked, and the image of her young patient faded. She looked into Aaron's dark blue eyes and saw both firmness and sympathy. Her panic receded.

"*Ja*," she said. "I can do this." She squared her shoulders and nodded at Daniel. "I have a bag in my cabin with some things I need. I'll be right back."

She dashed for her cabin, snatched up the duffel bag of emergency supplies she always kept on hand and ran back to the house. "Let's go," she told Daniel. Then she looked at Aaron, nodded her thanks and quipped, "Save some of the quiche for me."

Daniel wasted no time. He helped her into the buggy and handed up her bag, then swung himself into the driver's seat and took up the reins. The horse obediently backed up, turned around and took off down the road at a fast trot.

"How far apart are her contractions?" she asked the expectant father.

"About three minutes." The man focused on the road. "She's had two miscarriages in the past, but we have three healthy children, and she carried this one to term."

"Who helped deliver her other babies?"

"She went to the hospital with the last one because of the miscarriages, but before that her mother attended her. But her mother doesn't have any medical training, just a little bit of midwife experience. The moment Eva met you, she told me she'd hoped you could help her when the time came."

Miriam wondered why Eva hadn't asked for her help in advance. "Has she had any prenatal care?" she inquired.

"*Ja*, she sees a nurse in town regularly. But like most women in our church, she prefers to have her babies at home. It's also less costly and invasive." Daniel guided the horse around a curve in the road. "She meant to ask you to attend her beforehand, but her water broke unexpectedly a short time ago, and things moved very fast. A neighbor is watching our other children, and Eva's mother is with her now."

All in all, it sounded like a normal situation—nothing Miriam hadn't handled many times before. She would *not* think of her young patient. She would *not*.

After a few more minutes, Daniel pulled the horse to

a stop before a two-story farmhouse. Miriam quickly jumped out of the buggy. "I'll just go right in," she told the expectant father.

"*Ja, bitte.* I'll stable the horse and be right there."

Miriam entered the house, where an older woman emerged from the bedroom to meet her. "I didn't have the chance to meet you last week at church. I'm Anna Miller. My daughter is in there."

Miriam shook hands with her, then pushed into the bedroom, where Eva lay on a bed, panting. Miriam took a quick glance around the room. This was not a young woman having seizures due to drug addiction; this was a healthy mother tended to by her *mamm.* The bedroom was stocked with basic supplies already: clean linens, steaming water, a bassinet with tiny newborn clothes and diapers, even a scale for documenting birth weight.

"*Danke* for coming," said Eva with a weak smile. "It seems this little one is in a hurry to enter the world."

"Well, we'll make sure it arrives safe and sound," replied Miriam. She unzipped her duffel bag and rummaged for the supplies she needed, starting with a stethoscope to listen to the fetal heartbeat. "*Ach, ja.* The *boppli* is doing fine in there."

Miriam examined Eva and timed her contractions. Her professional confidence rose to meet the situation. In the vast majority of childbirths, the mother did most of the work. Miriam's job was to mitigate any problems and discern any true emergencies that would require medical intervention in a hospital. Eva showed none of those symptoms.

Instead, the labor progressed normally. Anna sat

by her daughter's side and wiped her forehead with a damp cloth.

Daniel entered the room, his eyes immediately drawn to his wife as a contraction hit. "Everything okay?" he asked Miriam anxiously.

"*Ja*, perfectly normal." Miriam smiled at the worried man. "You'll have another *boppli* very soon. Do you know if it's a boy or a girl?"

The man shook his head. "It's whatever *Gott* sees fit to send us," he replied simply. "We will love it no matter what."

The next hour brought Eva closer to delivering her baby. The room grew dark, and Daniel brought in enough oil lamps so Miriam could see clearly.

"That's *gut*," encouraged Miriam. "One more push, Eva. That should do it."

A short time later, Eva's baby was born.

"*Ach*, you have a beautiful little boy," said Miriam. She did a rapid evaluation on the newborn, and he came away with a perfect Apgar score.

"A boy," breathed Daniel, holding his wife's hand.

"A boy," Eva repeated, laughing through tears. *"Gott ist gut."*

"Another grandson," said Anna with a smile.

The room was full of quiet joy as Miriam attended to Eva's needs. *Mamm*, *dat*, and *grossmammi* rejoiced at the new life, cooing at the tiny infant. Miriam smiled at the family. Lit by soft lamplight, with Eva and the baby cleaned up, there was something almost spiritual about the tableau. "*Danke*, *Gott*," she whispered.

"Eli?" Daniel asked his wife.

"*Ja*, Eli." Eva cuddled the infant and glanced at Miriam. "It's the name we selected if *Gott* gave us a boy. Eli Joseph."

Miriam nodded with approval. "*Wunderbar.* Oh, Eva, he's beautiful."

"Ja." Eva dropped a kiss on the baby's forehead.

After half an hour, Miriam saw no other reason to stay. She gave a final examination of both her patients and was satisfied. Eva had no complications, and the baby was strong and healthy.

"I will drive you home," said Daniel as she packed up her medical supplies. "Words cannot express my gratitude for your helping Eva."

The new *dat* continued to express his thanks as the horse clip-clopped through the night, with side lanterns on the buggy to illuminate the way.

Later, back in her own cabin, she lay in bed, staring at the dark ceiling. She was tired but felt too keyed up to sleep.

Would *Gott* be angry that she had broken her own promise to Him? Despite her spiritual concerns, Miriam felt elated in the aftermath of the birth. Midwifery always did that for her—except for that one instance…

She rolled over and punched her pillow, trying to work through her conflict. Then a vision of Aaron rose before her. His dark blue eyes looked darker when he had shaken her shoulders a few hours ago. He had pierced through her fears. She had felt confidence and assurance flow into her as he jolted her out of her panic. He was quite a man.

Restless, she got out of bed, walked through the darkened cabin and settled in the rocker on the front porch, her muslin nightgown flowing around her legs. The stars overhead were gloriously bright. Crickets chirped. An owl hooted in a nearby tree. And a mile or two away, a family rejoiced in the birth of their new son.

Could she give this up? Could she give up her vocation—her calling—as a penance for losing that young patient? She had a sudden urge to discuss her conflict with someone. Again, the image of Aaron rose before her eyes.

More and more, she realized Aaron was on her mind.

Suddenly exhausted, she went back to bed. She whispered her prayers before falling asleep—and included a prayer for guidance and discernment. She needed both.

In the sudden silence following Miriam's departure to the Hostetlers', Aaron looked at Thomas and Emma. "Well, that changes everything, I suppose," he quipped.

Emma reseated herself and gestured toward him to follow suit. "I hope you still have a *gut* appetite."

"*Ja*, of course." Aaron sat down and forked up a bit of quiche. He chewed meditatively. "That was really something," he remarked. "Did you see the way she straightened up her shoulders and took up the challenge? She's quite a woman."

He caught a startled glance between Thomas and Emma, and he realized that such a comment could easily be misconstrued.

But his neighbors were good hosts, and they didn't say anything that might embarrass him. "She's always been that way—even as a child," Thomas said. "Miriam has a gentle heart, but she's got more steel inside her than almost anyone I know." He winked at his wife. "With one possible exception."

Aaron found himself with a burning desire to ask Thomas about his sister's youth but knew it wasn't his place. Miriam would tell him about herself in her own good time.

"I'm hoping Miriam will help with this little one when my time comes," said Emma, patting her mid-section. "We don't have a midwife in the community, and I know most women prefer not to use the hospital if they don't have to."

The intimacies of childbirth was not a topic he felt comfortable with. Instead, he tried his best to maintain a pleasant conversation with his neighbors without Miriam's bolstering presence. He knew his social skills were rusty, and he'd depended on Miriam to smooth the way. But then he remembered her words of advice.

Immediately, he turned to Emma. "Tell me about your soapmaking," he asked her.

Eyes sparkling, she launched into a detailed account of her business: her failed attempt to secure funding for a dedicated storefront; the enhanced exposure Thomas had helped her achieve at the mercantile in town, where he worked as a bookkeeper; and the widespread popularity of her products, not just within the church community but the whole town.

In her enthusiasm, she dominated the conversation for a good fifteen minutes, during which, Aaron made polite, encouraging remarks. When her recital was concluded, Aaron turned to Thomas. "How do you like having your own bookkeeping business?"

Thomas related how he had made the accounting at Yoder's Mercantile so efficient that he now only needed to work there two or three days a week; the rest of the time, he worked freelance, handling the books for a wide variety of Plain businesses in the area.

By the time both his hosts had exhausted their respective subjects, dinner was finished. The outside had darkened, and Thomas lit a lamp for the table. Emma served a delicate pudding pie for dessert, and Thomas made coffee. Leaning back in his chair, Aaron realized how much he enjoyed the company of his neighbors, even without Miriam there.

"Now, tell us about the farm," Thomas invited as they settled into comfortable chairs in the living room with cups of coffee. Hannah climbed into her father's lap, and he snuggled her close. "Miriam tells us you're amazingly self-sufficient."

"*Ja*, well, I had reason to be." Aaron made a vague gesture toward his face. "My thought was to make it so I never had to leave the farm. I realize now that's probably not the best course of action, but it… It kept me busy."

"Tell me about your root cellar," said Emma.

"Well, it was one of the first things I built, since I knew I would need it." Aaron relaxed into his chair. He remembered now this was how social engagements worked—each party asking questions of the other. "I showed Miriam the front part where I keep the cheese, but I have another section in back, curtained off, where I can store garden produce."

"Root cellars are rare out here," remarked Thomas. "I've often thought it would be a *gut* side business to get into, installing them for everyone."

"It was a bit of work," Aaron admitted. "The soil here has so much clay that drainage was a problem. Essentially, I had to make an artificial hill, burying the cinder block room with soil, and then put in French drains below."

Thomas shook his head. "Too much engineering for me," he remarked. "But then, Miriam said you have a knack for problem-solving. She said you're working on a device to milk cows one-handed?"

Just how much did Miriam talk about him to her brother and sister-in-law? Aaron found himself flattered to be the object of discussion, since apparently, none of it involved his appearance.

"*Ja*," he replied. He went on to let Thomas know what he had in mind for the one-handed milking device.

Thomas let out a low whistle. "You really do have an engineer's mind, Aaron. If you get this up and running, I can think of several older people who would use it because it's too painful to milk their animals anymore."

"It's something you should display at the Mountain Days Festival," remarked Emma. She rocked gently in her chair, one hand resting on her belly. "Uncle Samuel likes to showcase our church's talents, and I envision your booth having not just this milking device but all the other clever inventions you've created over the last few years."

Aaron managed an uneasy chuckle. "*Ja*, but who would man the booth?" he asked rhetorically. "It wouldn't be me."

"Why not?" Emma's voice was casual. "You're the most qualified to discuss everything, ain't so?"

"Because I don't want to be seen." In the past, he would have snapped the words; now, he softened them in the face of his neighbors and their genuine interest.

Emma gave him a gentle smile. "You probably won't

believe me when I say no one notices your scars after a few minutes, Aaron. All we see is the man underneath—the one who is so clever and accomplished that Miriam can't stop talking about you when she comes home in the evenings."

Aaron sat, stunned, staring at Emma. Miriam couldn't stop talking about him? He was burning to ask what she said, but he couldn't. His throat stopped working for a moment; then he was finally able to croak, "*Danke.*"

Thomas looked down at the child in his arms. Hannah's eyes were drooping. "I think someone's ready for bed," he remarked. "Are you ready for a story, *liebling*?"

"*Ja*," the child mumbled.

"I can help with the dishes," Aaron offered, rising and collecting his coffee cup.

"With one arm in a cast? You'll do nothing of the sort," Emma retorted.

"Then I should probably be going." He watched as Thomas lifted the sleepy five-year-old. The little girl snaked her arms around her stepfather's neck and laid her head trustingly on his shoulder. "*Danke*, both of you, for the dinner invitation. I enjoyed this evening very much."

"Don't be a stranger, Aaron." Emma rested a hand on her extended abdomen and gave him a warm smile. "You're an excellent neighbor, and we enjoyed your company."

"*Danke*," he repeated. "I hope everything went well at the Hostetlers, but I expect Miriam will fill us in tomorrow."

He took his leave and walked back to his farmhouse alone—yet not alone. The warmth of the evening's company sustained him. He was glad the Kemps were his neighbors.

And his heartbeat quickened. He still couldn't believe that Miriam talked about him so often.

Major bounded around the yard in excitement upon his return. The huge black dog was virtually invisible in the near darkness; it was easy to see how Miriam hadn't seen the animal the night she hit Aaron with her car. Aaron didn't remember much about that night—including how Major had escaped the yard—but he was glad his companion hadn't been injured. He ruffled the dog's ears with affection and let the animal precede him into the house.

He went about lighting some lamps and doing some of the easier evening tasks he could manage one-handed, all the while thinking about Miriam and wondering how Eva Hostetler was.

But his mind flopped back to Emma's words. Miriam couldn't stop talking about him? Really?

He realized Emma's casual comment filled him with a wild hope. Miriam was always on his mind. Could it be he was on her mind as well?

He couldn't wait to see her in the morning.

Chapter Eleven

Miriam woke the next morning, recalling Eva's successful birth the night before. She felt the warm glow she always felt after assisting in bringing a new life into the world.

Then she remembered she had violated her own promise to *Gott*. That brought her quickly back to earth. She had some apologizing to do to the Almighty.

And she was late. Miriam glanced at the clock and scrambled out of bed. Her stomach growled since she hadn't eaten dinner the night before, but there was no time to waste. Cows didn't like changes to their schedule.

She flung on her clothes, splashed her face with water, pinned up her hair and donned her *kapp*. Then she dashed out the door, practically running down the driveway, across the road and toward Aaron's house.

Aaron was at the kitchen table, tinkering with something, when she arrived. "Sorry I'm late," she apologized as she snatched the sterilized buckets from the kitchen counter. "I'm off to milk the cows."

"How did it go last night?"

"I'll tell you later." Buckets in hand, she headed toward the barn.

The cows were indeed restless, and Miriam forced herself to calm down. Cows had a tendency to pick up agitation in their human handlers, and she didn't want them kicking over buckets just because she'd overslept.

With efficiency, she brought the first animal into the milking stall and settled into her job. She heard a noise and looked over to see Aaron carrying the large milk can.

"You forgot this," he offered with a smile.

"*Ja, danke.* I'm sorry, I didn't mean to oversleep..."

"Don't worry about it. So how did it go last night?"

"It went great." She smiled. "Eva had a beautiful boy. But I didn't get home until late." She finished with one cow and poured the milk from the bucket into the milk can Aaron had brought in. Then she released the cow and clipped a lead rope onto the next animal to bring it into the milking stall.

"What did they name him?" inquired Aaron, standing by and watching her work.

"Eli Joseph. Isn't that lovely?"

"*Ja*, very nice. The Hostetlers, they're *gut* people."

"Eva is someone I'd like to get to know better."

"She's a nice woman." Aaron looked around the barn. "I'm going to start cleaning stalls," he offered. "I'm not as efficient with one arm, but I can manage well enough. Oh, and don't worry about the chickens. I've already taken care of them."

"Danke."

He went off to do his task. There was something comforting and companionable about having him work in the barn at the same time she was milking. He was managing more chores now, compensating for his limited movement in one arm by the partial use of his fingers. She found she enjoyed sharing the jobs with him.

Within half an hour, she'd poured the last of the milk into the milk can and released the cow to her calf. Aaron had finished cleaning the stalls. He trundled over the hand truck, and she slipped the heavy milk can onto the platform and strapped it in. Aaron took the buckets.

"Have you had breakfast?" she asked as she pushed the hand truck toward the house.

"*Ja*," he replied. "Emma sent me home with some of the quiche from last night. Have you eaten?"

"*Nein*. And I'll admit, I'm hungry since I didn't eat dinner last night."

"I have plenty of quiche left over. I'll heat it up while you strain the milk."

"*Danke*, Aaron." She smiled at him and was rewarded with a rare smile back.

She caught her breath. Really, under those scars, he was an extraordinarily handsome man. The morning sun shone in his dark blue eyes beneath his hat, and he smelled of soap and straw.

The Newfoundland broke her reverie. Major loped up, tongue lolling, and sniffed at the milk can. "Shoo, you big oaf," she said to the animal affectionately. She liked the huge canine.

At the kitchen door, she unstrapped the milk can; then she took one handle as Aaron took the other, and they hoisted the can into the kitchen.

"Sorry to leave you alone with Thomas and Emma last night," she said as she prepared to strain the milk.

Aaron slipped the leftover quiche into the propane oven to heat.

"It went fine," he said, and even managed a rusty chuckle. "Remember how you half joked that all I had to do was ask Emma about her soap business or Thomas about his bookkeeping, and they'd do all the talking? You were right."

She laughed. "Good for you."

"Emma did say she hoped you would help when it came time to have her own baby," he added.

The smile dropped from Miriam's face. "Oh…" she whispered without thinking.

Aaron looked at her sharply. "Why would you help Eva but not Emma?" he asked. "She's your *schwester-in-law*."

She took a ragged breath and concentrated on straining the milk. "I love her like a sister. What if something went wrong? What if something happened to her or the baby? I would never forgive myself."

"It seems you haven't forgiven yourself anyway," he said quietly. "You're highly skilled in a critical field. Is this something you should give up? Or something you even *want* to give up?"

Her hands stalled over the milk strainer, and tears filled her vision. "But I promised *Gott*."

"Miriam." Aaron touched her shoulder. "What can I say or do to convince you not to abandon your career?"

At his gentle question, Miriam felt the grief and failure well up inside her. He was right: she *hadn't* forgiven herself for losing that patient. As a result, she was certain *Gott* hadn't forgiven her either.

"I don't know." The words came out in a sob, then the floodgates opened.

Aaron led her to the kitchen table, where he gently helped her into a chair, pulled the other chair close and simply held her.

Miriam wept. She cried in ugly, incoherent sobs over the pain of losing both her young patient and the baby, as well as the grief of losing her vocation in exchange for forgiveness.

When the storm passed, she realized Aaron had pressed her into his chest, and his shirt was soaked with her tears. For a moment, she longed to stay where she was, with his arms around her and the hard cast pressing into her back. But it wouldn't be appropriate. She drew back and fumbled for the handkerchief in her apron pocket. She buried her face in the cloth. "Sorry," she mumbled.

"I think this was long past due," he remarked dryly. "But you never told me what happened. Everyone in the medical field must lose a patient from time to time. What was it about your experience that was so bad?"

She twisted the handkerchief in her hands, longing to answer his question. She realized she had bottled everything up for months now, until it had become the painful wound she often accused Aaron himself of nurturing.

She gave a shuddering sigh. "The young woman had been living on the streets. She couldn't have been older than sixteen. No prenatal care at all. We're estimating she was at thirty-four, thirty-five weeks of pregnancy, but we couldn't be sure. She wandered into the ER, having seizures. I was doing my ER rotation and was on duty at the time."

"Alone?"

"Skeletal staff. It was late at night, and a lot of the staff were working on three traumas from a bad car accident." She wrung the handkerchief. "I was the only one who could be spared to help this girl. And no matter what I did… No matter what I did…she didn't make it." She shivered and covered her face with her hands. "Dear *Gott*, she was so young…"

Aaron sat totally still, listening. "What did you do?"

"Everything, it seemed. Her blood pressure was sky high. Her seizures wouldn't stop, no matter what I tried. I was trying to monitor the fetus, and it just seemed that the poor baby was severely distressed. And I couldn't do anything about it." She drew a sobbing breath. "I punched the emergency button, tried to get more staff to help me, but they had dying patients to deal with, and no one could be spared."

"How can you triage when everyone's in the same boat?" he muttered.

"That's it exactly." A convulsive sob ripped through her before she controlled herself. "I finally realized that this was more than I could handle. I rushed her up to Obstetrics and had them alert the ob-gyn on call. But by then, it was too late. She went into cardiac arrest. And I couldn't help her. Couldn't help her…"

She sat slumped with her elbows on her knees, staring at the floor. After a moment, she concluded, "So I promised *Gott* to give up my medical career if only He could forgive me."

After a moment, Aaron said quietly, "I'm just a layperson, but it seems to me it wasn't your lack of skill that caused her death. If this poor girl was living on the streets, she was most likely ill and addicted to drugs. It sounds like you're blaming yourself for her death even though it wasn't your fault."

She sniffed. "Don't you think I've told myself that over and over again?"

"And you've convinced yourself *Gott* wants you to give up medicine in exchange for forgiveness?"

"*Ja.* I guess. It was the only sacrifice I could think of that was big enough to offer Him."

"Miriam, this sounds like something you should discuss with the bishop. But I'll say this—I don't think that's how *Gott* works."

"I will never give up on *Gott*," she said softly. "But I don't know why I'm so convinced He gave up on me. It's a feeling I can't shake."

Aaron was floored by that small, quiet statement. Did Miriam honestly think *Gott* ever gave up on someone?

Yet he stopped himself from chastising her. Hadn't he himself gone through similar doubts? Wasn't he still full of residual anger at the Almighty for what had happened to his face? Who was he to question Miriam's convoluted logic in her pursuit to keep *Gott*'s favor?

"So now you know," Miriam concluded with a sad, tearstained smile. She took a deep, shuddering breath. "And I guess you're right. I *have* been blaming myself and bottling this all up." She hiccupped. "I've never told a soul everything that happened that night or how much it messed me up, made me doubt my training."

"It helps sometimes, just to cry away the grief," he admitted.

She eyed him. "You have a powerful amount of sympathy, Aaron. I expect it's because you've been through your own Gethsemane. Since I've confessed my own dark sins, won't you tell me what happened to you?"

The request came as a shock to him. In the three years since the fire, he had never told anyone about it.

"Don't turn away," Miriam said quietly. "There's a reason the Bible emphasizes the importance of confession. Tell me what happened, Aaron."

Strangely, he felt a strong urge to do just what she'd asked. He slumped back down and pinched the bridge of his nose as the memories he'd tried so hard to push away came back.

"The fire started in a neighbor's barn," he murmured, almost in a whisper. "I heard the neighbors screaming as they tried to get all their animals out. I ran over to help, shooing horses away from the flames and releasing cows into a field. The smoke was very thick and made it hard to see. It—it seemed the whole structure was on fire. I was the last one in the barn when a burning beam fell on me and trapped me. That's all I remember. Later, my neighbor David told me he was able to shove the beam off me and d-drag me out. I woke up in the hospital, and there I stayed for a long time."

"Oh, Aaron..." whispered Miriam.

"The doctors did what they could," he continued, staring at the floor and recalling all those days lying in bed. "But no amount of plastic surgery helped. They were able to save the vision in my left eye and reshape my nose, but that was it. In the space of an instant, *Gott* saw fit to afflict me with the face of a monster."

She shook her head. "You're not a monster, Aaron. You know that."

"It's how I feel. Or felt. I've gotten used to it now. But no monster wants to be stared at."

"And that's why you moved to Montana?"

"Nein." He raised his eyes to her. "I moved because my betrothed, Denise, came to visit me in the hospital and told me she couldn't go through with the wedding."

Miriam sucked in her breath and stared at him, a shocked look on her face.

"It was a bitter blow," he went on. "In retrospect, it's probably *gut* the accident happened before the wedding and not after. I don't know what she would have done had she been bound to me for all eternity."

"Shallow twit," Miriam muttered.

He barked in humorless laughter. "*Ja*, maybe. I certainly saw into her soul at that moment and didn't like what I saw. I thought I knew her well—well enough to want to share my life with her—but it seems I was wrong."

"When she broke up with you, was she mean? Angry? Sad?"

He thought for a moment. "Determined, I guess," he replied. "She simply said she couldn't go through with the wedding. It was obvious why. In some ways, I'm more bitter about her abandonment than the accident," he admitted. "It confirmed what I already was thinking. That from then on, my life would be a constant parade of people withdrawing from me in one way or another."

"And *that*'s why you came to Montana." It was a statement, not a question.

"*Ja.* I left everything behind. I do miss my family at

times, but they understood. I came here because I had the opportunity to buy a farm for much cheaper than in Pennsylvania, plus the area had far less people. I had worked hard to save money for my future with Denise, so I used that money to buy this property. It's become my sanctuary. I can't quite claim I've come to dislike people, but I've come awfully close."

"Which is why you were determined to be so self-sufficient," Miriam added.

"*Ja.* I wanted solitude. I wanted to hole up and be left alone, to never see another soul unless I had to. I made that clear to the bishop when I first arrived."

"But you said everyone in this church community has been welcoming?"

"As welcoming as they could be." He shrugged. "There was still a lot of shock and surprise, a lot of averted faces and falsely bright, distracted chitchat. I've seen it all in the last three years and can spot that falseness from a mile away."

"It's a lonely path you've set for yourself."

"Maybe. And maybe it's the wrong path, but I couldn't figure out any other way to deal with the situation."

"Yet you had dinner with my brother and sister-in-law last night. Did you enjoy yourself?"

"*Ja.* In fact, I enjoyed myself very much. Do you know what Hannah did? She asked me to read her a story." The wonder of that request hit him again. "She climbed into my lap and listened to me read like I was any other person. She wasn't put off by my face at all."

"Hannah is a sweetheart," agreed Miriam. "But listen to me. You helped me through my own panic last night. You said I had to get back on the horse that bucked me. But don't you see…you're refusing to follow the very advice you gave me."

The last thing Aaron had expected was to have his own words thrown back in his face. Anger was an easy and familiar reaction. He got to his feet and glared at her. "It's different."

"No it's not." Miriam stood up as well. "Can't you hear yourself? How different is it for me to work through my fears if you won't work through yours?"

"That's easy for you to say. Your fears are hidden deep inside. My fears are right out in the open." He gestured toward his ravaged features. "You're not the one facing revulsion wherever you go."

"You are one of the cleverest and most original men I've ever met. Can't you see your own skills and unique contributions to the church community?" she responded.

"*Nein.* All I can see is the false cheerfulness as women avert their eyes and children refuse to come near me."

"Then you're not giving anyone the opportunity to get to know you. That's on you, Aaron, not anyone else. *Ja*, it's a bit of a shock when someone first sees you. That lasts, oh, about thirty seconds. After that, their impression of you depends entirely on how you behave back toward them. The more you growl and glare, the more people will stay away. But did Hannah stay away from you last night, or did she accept you as you are?"

He stared at her, trying to deny the truth of what she said and summon the familiar anger that he had clung to for so long. He heard the clock ticking in the silence.

Miriam gave him what could only be a smug smile.

"Think about it, Aaron." She turned. "I'll be back in a few hours to do the evening chores."

She patted Major, who was sitting in a corner of the kitchen, and then she left, the kitchen door clicking closed behind her.

Aaron dropped back down into his chair. The clock continued to tick. A rooster crowed. Birds twittered. But he was alone—as he wanted it.

Or did he? Was being alone truly what he really wanted?

Maybe the time for being alone had passed. Maybe the solitude had done its job and healed him.

He found himself shaken by Miriam's praise. Is that how she saw him? Clever and original? Enough that she couldn't stop talking about him when she was with her brother and sister-in-law?

One thing he knew for certain: Miriam had never recoiled from him. She had even kissed him on the cheek yesterday. He was worried he was becoming unhealthily fixated on her simply because she was the first woman who had treated him normally since the accident.

Or was she? Was he too busy scaring people away with his growls and glares that he rebuffed any overtures of friendship and fellowship? When he worked with other men on communal carpentry projects—building a barn or a home—his self-consciousness about his appearance faded in the overall task of swinging a hammer and joining boards. Certainly, the men he worked with had never treated him any differently during those projects.

But neither did they seek him out for companionable moments outside of work.

Because he wouldn't let them? Was his desire for solitude becoming a self-fulfilling prophecy simply because he pushed everyone away before they could hurt him?

It was a lot to think over.

Chapter Twelve

Miriam left Aaron's farm and marched straight to the bishop's home, just a quarter mile down the road. She needed the church leader's help with something.

The bishop's wife, Lois, was working in her garden. She straightened up and shaded her eyes as Miriam approached. "*Guder mariye*, Miriam," the older woman said with some surprise. "Beautiful day, *ja*?"

"*Ja*," agreed Miriam. "I'm sorry to drop in unexpectedly, but is your *hutband* home? I have an issue I'd like to discuss with him."

"He's out back. Would you like to sit on the porch and I'll get him?"

"Danke." Miriam mounted the steps to the pleasantly shaded porch positioned to take advantage of the view while Lois made her way to the back of the house.

After a few moments, Bishop Beiler came into sight. "*Guder mariye*, Miriam," he said, his eyes a bit anxious. "Is there a problem?"

"*Ja*, but not an urgent one," she replied. "Do you have a few minutes to talk?"

"*Ja*, sure." He addressed his wife. "*Lieb*, would you mind bringing us some lemonade?"

Lois nodded and headed into the house while the bishop gestured toward two wicker rocking chairs flanking a small table. Miriam seated herself in one chair while the bishop lowered his lanky form into the other.

"*Danke*," she said when Lois set two glasses of lemonade on the table. She waited until the bishop's wife had discreetly retreated to her garden.

"I've just come from Aaron's," Miriam began. "Something rather extraordinary happened. He told me the circumstances behind the accident that disfigured his face. But that's not why I'm here. Instead, I need your help."

"Of course," the bishop replied, his eyes bright with curiosity.

"I need help drawing him out of his shell," Miriam stated. "He's admitted he has set up his farm so as to never have to see another soul. As you know, he was forced to accept my help after his arm was broken, but he wasn't happy about it. However, he's starting to soften up. To be honest, Bishop Beiler, I think he's ready to return to the wider world—and by that, I mean wider than just the church community, who has treated him very well."

The bishop rubbed his chin. "I believe I've been remiss in this instance," he said. "I felt I was honoring Aaron's request for privacy, when in fact what he really needed was more socialization."

"I don't think you've been remiss at all," returned Miriam. "He needed his solitude—he truly did. I've worked with a number of burn patients in my career, and withdrawing from society is very normal. They need time to adjust, time to mourn the loss of what they were before their burns. But for Aaron, it's been three years. I think he's finally accepted that he'll never look like he did before the accident. Now it's time to get him out of isolation and return to the real world."

The older man stared at his glass of lemonade with a pensive face. "I'm trying to think what he might do outside of church activities," he said after a moment. "He seems perfectly willing to join us whenever we have a house or barn to build, and he never skips church services. But to the best of my knowledge, he rarely goes to town and seldom mingles with the *Englisch*. We're a small-enough community, and Pierce is a small-enough town that it's important to be on *gut* terms with the *Englisch*..." He thought a moment longer, then snapped his fingers. "Mountain Days!"

Miriam was bewildered for a moment, then she remembered. "That's the town's yearly celebration, isn't it?"

"*Ja.* They have a big party. The whole town participates, and it brings in a lot of visitors from elsewhere too. There's a parade—there are arts and crafts exhibits, livestock exhibits, even a small carnival with rides and such. It's a lot of fun. A couple years ago, the committee that puts it on came to me and asked the church to participate by putting on a demonstration of our collective skills. We did, and it was a great success, and it helped enormously in terms of public relations. We've done it ever since. Everyone had booths or demo areas showcasing various Amish skills. I could encourage Aaron to get involved in that."

"I wonder..." Miriam tapped her chin thoughtfully. "He's working on this *wunderbar* invention, a device that will let him milk cows one-handed. He's got a rough prototype right now and planned to bring it to a machinist to get some of the details worked out. He's remarkably innovative and has quite a number of other inventions he's created. Could he have a booth to showcase them?"

"That's an excellent idea," the older man said. "Mountain Days takes place in late August, so he would have enough time to pull everything together."

"And he wouldn't have to man it alone," added Miriam, smiling at the prospect. "I'd be happy to be there too. Maybe Emma can showcase her soaps as well."

"She already has her own booth, but nothing says her booth and Aaron's booth can't be side by side." The bishop's eyes twinkled. "Though her baby will have been born by then, so we'll see if she wants to attend."

Miriam gave him a huge grin. "*Danke*, Bishop Beiler. I've been gently trying to persuade Aaron to get out more, but there's only so much I can do. But you're the church leader. He respects you. I figure you have a lot more clout than I do when it comes to what is, after all, a very sensitive subject for him." She fiddled with her glass of lemonade. "Also, ah...you may not want to mention my part in this."

He chuckled. "*Nein*, don't worry. The only one who will know of this is my wife, from whom I keep no secrets. Leave everything to me. And *danke* for watching out for Aaron, Miriam. I'm glad he has you for a friend."

For the first time, Miriam recognized that her request to the bishop might be misconstrued as something more than friendship. Her cheeks heated. "He's a *gut* man," she told him.

"*Ja*, he is. Very well. Mountain Days, here we come." He rose out of his chair.

Miriam took the hint and finished her lemonade. "*Danke*," she said, getting out of her rocking chair as well. "Let me know if there's anything I should do."

"I will."

Miriam said her farewells to Lois, then walked down the road toward Emma and Thomas's house. She found her sister-in-law and niece in the kitchen, making a batch of soap. "Mmm, smells like mint in here," she noted.

"Spearmint!" announced Hannah, holding up some of the plant as she stripped leaves off the stems. "My favorite!"

Miriam chuckled and kissed the child's head. "Lemon is my favorite soap your *mamm* makes."

"Did you just come from Aaron's?" inquired Emma, stirring a pot on the propane stove.

"*Nein*, I just came from seeing your uncle." Miriam explained the nature of her request to the church leader.

Emma paused her stirring, turned and stared in astonishment. "What a *gut* idea!" she exclaimed. "I suggested the same thing yesterday evening after you left to deliver Eva's baby, but it never occurred to me to enlist *Onkel* Samuel to help persuade him." Then her gaze sharpened. "Is that the *only* reason you went to see my uncle?"

Miriam had an uneasy sense of what her sister-in-law was hinting at. "Is *what* the only reason?"

"Is there a deeper reason you're interested in helping Aaron come out of his shell?"

"Maybe." Miriam twiddled with the bundles of slightly wilted spearmint lying on the table. She knew exactly what Emma was asking. "I like Aaron. He's kind and interesting, and he has a brilliant mind. But he's stubborn. And I think he's still clinging to victimhood because he's too scared to go out."

Emma nodded but said nothing more as she turned back to the stove and resumed stirring. "We very much enjoyed having him to dinner last night. What a shame you couldn't be here during most of it, but I'm glad you helped Eva and her baby."

"I wonder..." Miriam paused in her absentminded crushing of the spearmint leaves. "Do you think I'm now somehow using Aaron as a replacement for my nursing career? I—I admit, I'm feeling adrift at the moment, without the anchor of my work, and using Aaron as a replacement."

"Well, if you are, there's no harm," said Emma briskly. "If it helps Aaron and it helps you, it's all *gut*. Your skills aren't going anywhere if you put them on hold for a little while."

But for how long? That was the question Miriam couldn't answer. She had bargained with *Gott* to give up those skills forever. The thought left her feeling bleak and unmoored.

But oddly, breaking down in front of Aaron that morning when she'd confessed the traumatic event that had led to that promise—losing her young patient—had helped. Was giving up her career truly what *Gott* wanted her to do?

It was too much to think about at the moment. Instead, she turned to her sister-in-law and said, "What can I do to help? I've never made soap before."

Staying distracted was far easier than examining painful insights.

Three days later, Aaron sat at his kitchen table with the prototype of the one-handed milking machine in front of him. Jonathan Zook, the church's machinist, had given him the rough components of the pump unit that created the suction. Aaron planned to wait until Miriam arrived for the evening chores to enlist her assistance in trying the device out.

So when he heard a knock at the door, he was a bit surprised. Miriam seldom bothered to knock anymore; plus, she always came in through the back door, not the front. "Come in!" he called out.

To his utter astonishment, the bishop poked his head inside the door. "*Guder nammidaag*, Aaron."

Aaron scrambled to his feet. "*G-guder nammidaag*, Bishop," he stammered. "I wasn't expecting you."

"*Ja*, I apologize for coming over unannounced, but I had something I wanted to discuss with you. Ah, what a *gut* boy…" Major rose from his dog bed and lumbered over to greet the visitor.

Aaron watched closely to make sure the gigantic canine didn't overwhelm the older man, but the dog behaved well.

"Won't you sit down?" he invited. "I don't have any lemonade, but I could offer you a glass of sun tea."

"*Ja, danke.*" Samuel Beiler removed his hat and mopped his brow. "It's a warmer afternoon than I anticipated."

Aaron opened the icebox to remove the jar of tea he'd brewed the day before. His hand shook as he poured. What did the bishop want?

"Nice place you have," Samuel said, glancing around. "I've never been in the house before."

"Danke." Aaron placed the glass of tea on the table. "To be honest, it was something of a mess until Miriam got her hands on it. Amazing what a difference a woman's touch can make."

"*Ja*, for sure and certain." Samuel sipped his tea, then focused on the milking device on the table. "What's this?"

"Something I've been experimenting with." Aaron sat back down and picked up the milker. "See? I've been designing something that would allow people with limited mobility in their hands to still milk their cows—or goats, for that matter. This part fits over the cow's quarter. When I pump this handle—" he demonstrated "—it should create a vacuum, which should draw the milk out into the jar. In theory, I only need to pump the handle once or twice, and the suction does the rest."

The bishop peered at the device for a few moments, then nodded. "Excellent," he pronounced. "A very nice idea. I've heard Emma talking about it. And in fact, this is why I came to visit today."

Aaron was surprised. "Because of the milking machine?"

"Partially, *ja*. But you have a number of small devices you've created over the last few years, all designed to offer shortcuts or solve a problem on a farm. What I would like you to do is bring together everything you've done and display them at a booth at the Mountain Days Festival in August."

Aaron could almost feel himself shrinking away from the older man. "*Nein*," he said flatly. "That would have to mean I'd be out among the *Englisch*. They wouldn't look at my inventions—they'd look at my face."

"*Ja*, they might," the bishop agreed. "For a moment or two. Then all you have to do is smile and explain about the devices you've made, and I guarantee you they'll want to hear about them. That's just the way people work."

"It's not that easy."

"Why not? When is the last time you tried it?"

The question stumped Aaron for a moment. He sputtered, "Well... Well..."

"Please, Aaron, I would consider it a personal favor if you would have a booth at the event," the bishop said gently. "Miriam or Emma could be there for some moral support, if you like. But this—" he touched the prototype "—as well as your other inventions show a side of our church community that I want the *Englisch* to see. They tend to lump us as quaint throwbacks to an earlier age, incapable of innovation or creativity, and you're a prime example of how that isn't the case."

"But... But..."

The bishop plowed on. "Do you know Lois, my *frau*, has been raving about the chicken feeders you made for her? The birds hardly waste any feed now that we're using the device you created. You have a brilliant mind, Aaron. I don't think I've ever met anyone as clever at solving problems or creating solutions. You're a credit to our church, and I would very much appreciate it if you would help represent us to the *Englisch* in town."

Compliments were so rare among the Amish that Aaron hardly knew what to say. Were his little inventions really that appreciated?

"So…can I count on you?" concluded the bishop with a smile.

"*J-ja*, sure," Aaron said weakly. What else could he say?

"*Danke*," the bishop said simply. He took another sip of tea. "We'll make it as comfortable as possible for you, even to the point of placing your booth in a less-exposed location among other booths. Benjamin Troyer is the one in charge of organizing it, so I'll let him know you've agreed to participate. *Ach*, Aaron, I appreciate this. I truly do."

Aaron nodded, his mind racing. He had to fight the urge to hide, to disappear. Facing a crowd of *Englisch* strangers filled him with dread…

Then he thought of Miriam. He calmed down. Thoughts of her were like cool water to a thirsty man. She would stand by him. She would help him get through the ordeal.

"I—I guess it would be *gut* for me," he admitted reluctantly. "Maybe I've been alone for too long."

"Perhaps." This bishop regarded him with a warm expression in his blue eyes. "You've been through a lot, but you're too *gut* a man to hide away forever. I think everyone in our church would be delighted to see you at the festival. Sometimes having a cheering squad helps, *ja*?"

"*Ja.*" Aaron realized the only cheering squad he needed—or wanted—was Miriam.

The bishop drained his glass of tea and stood up. "I'll

talk to Benjamin next time I see him. I'm sure he'll want to discuss specifics with you about what kind of booth you'll need, where it will be placed, that kind of thing." The bishop touched the milking prototype on the table. "And this will be very popular, I'm sure."

After the bishop left, Aaron sat at the table, a bit stunned at the turn of events. He wondered how much of the bishop's acclaim was just a ploy to get him to agree to the festival, but he dismissed the thought. Samuel Beiler wasn't known for duplicity.

But was he right? Would the *Englisch* stare at him for only a moment and then ignore his scars while they focused on his inventions?

Tentatively, he touched the left side of his face. He hadn't looked at himself in years—he refused to own a mirror of any kind. He wondered how bad he really looked. He felt the thickened skin, the twists and turns of healed epidermis where the burning beam had fallen on him. The scars extended from temple to chin, though, thankfully, it had spared his eye; he had full vision on both sides. His left ear and hearing were also undamaged.

Dropping his hand, he sighed. He didn't need a mirror to know he was hideous. And now the bishop wanted him to purposely expose himself to the *Englisch*, who would either avoid him, avert their eyes or engage in senseless, distracting chatter in an effort to pretend they didn't notice his disfigurement.

Unless…unless he took the bishop's advice: *he had to smile.*

Smiling was foreign to him now. He did it all the time with his animals, who never minded the lopsided result or the twisted caricature. But he seldom smiled at people.

And yet he recalled that time after church a few weeks ago, when Miriam had silently invited him to eat lunch with the Kemp family. Spontaneously, he had smiled at her in gratitude, and he had seen the wonder in her face when he did so. Then, later, when she had caught him laughing at Major's antics, she had recommended he smile more often.

Could it be that his smile wasn't as hideous as he thought?

He remembered what he was like before the accident; he knew he'd been handsome then. He knew his smile held some charisma. It was how he had attracted Denise, who seemed to have liked his appearance—perhaps overly much. Maybe that's why *Gott* saw fit to take away his looks and humble his pride.

But he could still smile… And if Miriam's reaction was anything to go by, then perhaps that still held some value.

Miriam. At the thought of her, a genuine smile flitted across his face. He was trying very hard not to admit just how preoccupied he was with her. He knew he could never compete with anyone, should another man become interested in courting her. In fact, he expected her unmarried status to be temporary here in Pierce.

The smile disappeared. And when the inevitable day came when she would marry, he would attend the wedding and wish her well, then return to his lonely cabin and mourn the loss.

But for the time being, he would enjoy her company while he could—including her presence at this dreaded booth at the Mountain Days Festival. She would help him get through it. And he *would* go through with it—not for the bishop, not for the church…but for Miriam.

Chapter Thirteen

"So then he talked me into it," concluded Aaron in the gloomiest voice possible, relating his conversation with Bishop Beiler the day before.

It was all Miriam could do to keep from pumping her fist in victory. Good for the bishop! She made a note to thank him next time she saw him.

But she kept her expression sympathetic. "I'd be happy to work the booth with you," she offered. "I can act as a buffer. Honestly, Aaron, I don't think it will be as bad as you imagine. It's as the bishop said—people may stare for a moment, but your inventions are so clever, I'm certain they'll just want to find out more about them."

"Well, I guess I'll find out. I don't plan to sell anything but will just have examples of the kinds of things I've put together."

"It's a demonstration of our collective skills more than anything, Thomas says—though a few people have items to sell. Emma sold a lot of her soap last year, for example. But this year, she may not attend, since she'll have had her baby by then. But I think you may want to have a few things stashed away for sale. Those chicken feeders, for instance. Who wouldn't want a feeder that doesn't waste food?"

"Maybe." He looked doubtful.

The Newfoundland walked up to Aaron and nudged his hand. Miriam watched the expression on his face lighten as he turned to the dog. "*Ja*, I *did* promise you, didn't I?"

"Promise him what?" she inquired.

"To take him to the pond and let him swim. It's warm today, and this big oaf loves nothing more than to splash in the water."

Miriam rubbed her chin. "I'm curious to see more of your property," she ventured. "May I go too?"

He looked surprised, then pleased. "*Ja*, of course! I'm sorry—I've never given you a tour of the rest of the property, have I?"

"*Nein*, and your farm is beautiful. I'd love to see it."

"Then let's go." With enthusiasm, he snatched his straw hat hanging on the back of the kitchen chair and placed it on his head.

With Major frolicking between them—it really did seem like the gigantic dog knew where they were headed—Miriam followed Aaron out of the house and beyond the barn.

He stopped and pointed to the pasture, where the cows were grazing. "I have fifty acres," he said. "The pasture is fairly small—only fifteen acres—but I need the rest for hay. The pasture is cross-fenced into five-acre plots so I can rotate. During the hottest part of the summer, I also let the cows into the woods to let them graze there since it offers them more shade. Plus, it keeps the grass trimmed."

"Nice." She knew just how much thought, planning and work he had put into his farm. The fencing alone was a formidable task.

He led her farther out onto the land. "Here are the pastures I mow for hay," he said. The broad fields rippled gently in the breeze. "It's a timothy-brome mix, and frankly it's just about ready to mow and bale. I may enlist your aid in getting the horses harnessed, but I think at this point, it's a task I can handle, even with limited mobility in one arm."

"I've helped my parents with the haying many a year," she reminded him. "It's not something I'm unfamiliar with—though of course I was never in charge, since I was a teenager at the time."

"Danke." He turned and smiled his rare smile. "Your help would make things easier," he admitted.

She nearly caught her breath. His smile literally transformed his face. She tried not to stare at him.

"Whenever you want to mow, just let me know," she said.

"Ja, danke." Appearing unaware of her turmoil, he continued walking. "It's been a *gut* summer for hay, and I should have plenty to get me through the winter and maybe a bit of extra to sell."

He led the way toward the edge of the forest. Unlike the woods of Indiana, these woods in Montana were primarily coniferous. The tall, stately trees made a dense canopy of shade. The ground under her feet became soft from the carpet of pine needles.

"I have to manage the woodlot carefully," he explained. "Firewood is one of the most abundant commodities to purchase around here since many of the *Englisch* use woodstoves too. But my goal is to always be able to harvest enough from my own land in a sustainable fashion. As it stands, most of these trees are growing too close together, so thinning them will be beneficial in the long run."

"How many cords do you use over the winter?"

"About four. I have an efficient stove, the cabin is small and its thick walls keep it well insulated. I don't see a problem in pulling four or five cords of wood out of the woodlot each year."

She paused and rested a hand on the trunk of a tree. "A lot of work," she remarked.

"But satisfying." He gazed around the forest. "I never realized just how satisfying it was to be completely self-sufficient—so I guess you could say that's one silver lining to the whole accident. It's a challenge, and one I enjoy tackling."

"But you must make *some* purchases," she inquired.

"Propane is probably my biggest expense," he replied. "You saw the five-hundred-gallon tank near the house. It's so much cooler to use a propane stove in the warmer months than the wood cookstove. But I earn enough from selling cheese and hay and other commodities to more than pay for the propane, as well as property taxes and other expenses. Besides, I don't go through much. I haven't had to refill the tank since I installed it, though I'll probably have it topped off before winter."

She shook her head. "Amazing."

"I think buying this farm was *Gott*'s doing," he said

quietly, gazing out at the woods. "He was offering me a refuge from the world after the accident, and I promised Him I would take *gut* care of it."

Just then, Major flopped onto the ground and gave a long-suffering sigh. Aaron chuckled. "Okay, you big goofball. Let's go to the pond."

He led the way along the edge of the woods, then followed the fence line back toward the pasture where the cows grazed. A grove of conifers shaded the edge of a small body of water a hundred feet across, with a lone chair at the edge. To Miriam, the single seat seemed significant. Aaron was used to thinking in terms of solitude.

"Watch this," he chuckled. He reached below the chair and picked up a toy, which he flung into the water.

Major went crashing after it, his huge body splashing into the water and creating small waves that lapped the shore. Miriam laughed at the sight.

"For sure and certain, he loves the water. Here, have a seat." He dusted off some pine needles and offered her the chair.

Miriam sat and watched while Aaron played with his dog, throwing the toy into the water over and over. He laughed and smiled and encouraged the canine's instinctive behavior.

She could hardly keep her eyes off him. He was like another man. His dark blue eyes sparkled, his teeth shone, his face was lit up with the pure joy of watching his beloved dog at play. She had never seen him so lighthearted and animated.

While Aaron threw the toy for the dog, she realized her feelings about him had changed from an obligation to a delight. She enjoyed working with him. She better understood the creative mind behind the scarred facade. She looked forward to the time she spent in his company.

And it seemed he was, at last, coming out of his shell. His laughter lit up his face in a way that transcended the disfigurement. She was starting to understand what his former fiancée had seen in him. He must have been positively charismatic before the accident.

All this led her toward a conclusion she wasn't quite ready to examine.

In some ways, Aaron was like one of her medical patients. She had never become personally involved with anyone she had cared for in the hospital, though she knew some nurses who had. Medical issues left people emotionally vulnerable, and it was easy to let that vulnerability lead to something more.

But as a nurse, she had always prided herself on her professionalism. Aaron technically wasn't her patient—but certainly, he was the first one who had pierced the layer of brisk efficiency she had built up and touched the heart underneath. It was marvelous to watch his struggles and journey from an injured, bitter man into the carefree individual she was watching now.

But throwing the toy for the dog was just an interlude, she knew. He always seemed to let his guard down when it came to his animals.

Could he ever let his guard down with her? Or did he see her simply as a person who had assisted him while he was unable to work his farm?

She didn't know. At the moment, it seemed presumptuous to ask. But she found herself more and more interested in the answer.

* * *

"Look at him go!" Aaron laughed with pure unadulterated joy as Major seized the toy and returned it once again to shore. There was something about the huge goofy dog that Aaron absolutely loved. The animal was in his element in the water, swimming with powerful strokes to "rescue" the floatie each time.

"He sure does love the water," agreed Miriam.

Major dropped the toy at Aaron's feet and looked up at him, dripping and panting, eager to go into the water again. Aaron flung the toy in a different direction in the pond, and Major went after it.

"Newfoundlands are amazing dogs," he told her. "They have a double-thick coat and webbed paws, so they're very *gut* at swimming. They even swim differently than other dogs. They move their legs in a down-and-out motion, like this." He demonstrated with his uncasted arm. "This gives them more power to every stroke. They can be trained for water rescues, but they often rescue people without any training at all. It seems to come naturally to them."

Major returned with the toy, and Aaron flung it into the water once again. Then Aaron came and flopped down on the grass next to the chair where Miriam sat. "Isn't he beautiful?"

"*Ja*," she replied. "How long have you had him?"

"About two and a half years. Since just after I came to Montana. The sad thing is, Newfoundlands don't have a very long lifespan. Ten years is the average, so I'll enjoy him while I can."

"You're so *gut* with animals, Aaron."

As he watched his dog, he grinned. "Major has gotten me through many lonely days and nights. All my animals have."

Miriam laughed as the dog lumbered to the shore, dropped the toy and shook water off himself with exaggerated movements. The animal was panting. "Does he know when he's had enough?" she teased. "Or will he keep going until he drops?"

"Probably both. C'mon, you big lug. Let's take a break." Aaron patted the ground in front of him, and the dog collapsed, looking very pleased with himself.

For a few moments, there was silence except for the dog's heavy breathing. Birds twittered in the trees above them. Aaron felt at peace. He hadn't laughed—truly laughed—with someone else for years. For just a little while, he'd felt like the handsome youth he used to be, and Miriam was a pretty woman whose interest he'd caught.

"I like it here," Miriam commented at last. He glanced up and saw she was gazing out across the pond and beyond, to the pasture where the cows grazed peacefully. "Montana is very different from Indiana, but it's beautiful here."

"I hope you stay," he ventured. The simple statement barely scratched the depths of the feeling behind it. He wanted Miriam to stay forever.

"I can't see why I would leave," she replied. "It's so *gut* to see my brother settled so happily. I—I just have to decide what to do once you no longer need me to milk your cows."

Aaron looked up at Miriam and locked eyes with her. The moment lengthened until he skittered his gaze away. "You'll think of s-something," he stuttered.

"You've only been here a little while. In another couple weeks, I'll get this cast off, and then I can milk my own cows."

"Don't be so sure," she replied lightly. "It will take some time to regain the strength in your arm, especially for something like milking. I just figure I'll stay on for a few weeks after the cast is removed, just in case."

While delighted with this development, Aaron wondered what motivated it. He didn't dare hope it was because Miriam was searching for an excuse to remain near him. He would never presume something like that.

A cloud of depression threatened to descend on him as he contemplated that idea. Three years ago, even while courting Denise, the attention of a woman would indicate only one thing: personal interest. But now? No. It was something he couldn't accept.

Yet beneath Miriam's medically motivated concerns, it seemed she had no problem being around him.

Human nature warred with the reality of his facial disfigurement. He refused to allow himself to build fantasies around Miriam. No matter how much she might smile and even laugh with him, it was a far cry from the courtship he once had and the future he'd once hoped for.

"You've gone so quiet," she remarked after a few moments.

"Just thinking," he returned.

"About what?"

He decided on partial honesty. "Oddly enough, about Denise," he replied. "I was wondering what she would have done had the accident happened *after* our wedding, not before."

"You mean, how would she have reacted to you?"

"Ja."

"Hmm. I've seen it go both ways," she said. "Sometimes, a bad accident will bring a married couple closer together. Other times, the chasm between them grows wide and they get divorced. What do you think would have happened with the two of you?"

"I don't know, but I strongly suspect the latter," he said. "But because divorce isn't possible in our church, I don't know what we would have done. I guess that's one of the silver linings in this very dark cloud," he added. "I was bitter about it for a long time, but it showed me she was a little more shallow than I realized. To be fair, I used to be very handsome. I'm sure that was part of her attraction to me."

"You're still much more handsome than you give yourself credit for, Aaron." Miriam's words were gentle. "When you smile and laugh the way you were doing a few minutes ago, it's almost impossible to notice the scars. You have one of the most captivating smiles I've ever seen."

Aaron stared at her. Her eyes were merry, twinkling in the dappled sunshine, as she looked back at him.

Handsome? No, he wasn't. He knew he wasn't. She was just being kind.

Yet he had to admit, he didn't even know what he looked like anymore. He didn't know how his smiles impacted his scars, since he refused to ever look in a mirror. Did Miriam see something he didn't?

So he panicked. Jumping to his feet, he said, "Um, it's getting late. I suppose we should head back."

He knew he was running away in an almost literal

fashion, but he couldn't bear the thought of a one-sided interest with Miriam. Or *was* it one-sided? It almost... seemed it wasn't. And that scared him even more.

"*Ja*, it's getting late," she agreed, and he got the distinct impression she was amused.

He didn't care. He needed to get away, to be alone, to process emotions that seemed too raw and powerful.

He kept the conversation on strictly neutral subjects as they walked back to the cabin, and with relief, he watched her walk away after she promised to be back for the afternoon chores. Collapsing onto his one comfortable reading chair in the living room, he stared at the wall of books across from him. Major, still damp from his swim, flopped down with a sigh at his feet.

Maybe it was just because he had been contemplating the contrast, but he knew Denise, whom he had once loved—with whom he'd once hoped to share the rest of his life—simply hadn't had the depth of feeling or understanding that Miriam did. He knew he was becoming romantically attracted to Miriam.

And it terrified him to think she might—just might—return the sentiment a little bit.

Because realistically, what could he do about it? The self-doubt that had never touched him before the accident now threatened to shut the door forever on his blossoming interest in the woman. If, wonder of wonders, Miriam somehow had developed feelings for him, could he believe her? Could a beauty ever fall in love with a beast?

Unlike the fairy tale, he had no hopes of ever returning to the handsome man he'd once been. After Denise's rejection, he had set up in his mind that no woman could ever overlook his scars and see the lonely man underneath.

But it seemed Miriam had. Perhaps it was the nurse in her, but it seemed she could do the impossible and look past the disfigurement to his core. And that scared him.

Could he even be thinking about building a life with her? Or would she, too, grow dissatisfied with his appearance? Would her eyes stray to a more handsome, unblemished man?

It was too big a risk to take. His heart had been shattered before; he wasn't sure he could go through it again. No, it was far better to keep Miriam at a distance, to admire her in every possible way but never admit his feelings for her.

This was his reality.

Chapter Fourteen

In the two weeks since Miriam had walked with Aaron and his dog to the pond, she had done a lot of long, hard thinking.

There was something about him that touched her. Seven weeks ago, when she'd accidentally hit Aaron with her car, he had been a bitter, withdrawn man—angry at the world in general and her in particular. Now he seemed calmer, more at peace. A little part of her hoped she'd had a hand in that transformation.

But she said nothing to him about her growing interest. Aaron was healing both physically and emotionally, but as a trained medical professional, she knew she couldn't push him. Besides, there was no hurry.

"I'll bet you can't wait to get the cast off," she observed as she strained the morning's milk. "Today's the big day! I'm kind of surprised the doctor gave you an appointment so late in the afternoon, but it won't take long to remove the cast."

Aaron was pouring the last few days' worth of dairy into pots, preparing to make cheese. "*Ja*, I'll be very glad to get this off," he replied. "It's awkward. And itchy! *Danke* for arranging to drive me to the appointment in your brother's rig."

"Of course. And—"

An urgent knock interrupted their conversation. Miriam glanced at Aaron and saw surprise on his face, but he strode over to the front door and opened it.

Thomas stood there, panting a bit, a desperate look on his face. "Miriam, Emma's in labor," he said without preamble. "Can you help?"

For just a moment, she stood rooted to the spot. She'd known this day would come. She had tried urging her sister-in-law to go to the local hospital, but Emma would have none of it—not when there was a highly qualified nurse–midwife living on their own farm.

"Miriam, please…" said Thomas.

Aaron walked over to her. As before, he took her by the shoulders and gave her a little shake. "You'll do fine," he told her in a low voice. "Nothing will go wrong. Emma is a strong and healthy woman. You can do this." He leaned in and kissed her, briefly, on the cheek.

His touch jolted her. Miriam snapped out of her trance. She looked into his dark blue eyes and saw strength.

"*Ja*," she said. Looking at her brother, she added, "Let's go."

They hurried down the driveway and across the road while Thomas explained to her that little Hannah was staying at the Beilers'.

"How far apart are her contractions?" asked Miriam.

"*Ach*, I don't know. All I know is she had me hurry

Hannah over to the Beilers, then asked me to rush over here and get you."

"Emma's no fool, and she's been through this before." Miriam did some hasty calculations in her head. "I'm guessing she's closer to her time than you think."

Thomas burst into the house with Miriam close on his heels. The place was tidy, as if Emma had wanted a clean house when the baby came. Thomas led the way toward the bedroom.

"There y-you are," panted Emma, leaning against a dresser. She wore a loose muslin nightgown. Her face was strained, but she smiled at Miriam. "I knew you'd come."

Miriam took charge. "Thomas, make sure there's a pot of water boiling. Emma, give me a couple minutes—I'm going to get my midwife bag from the cabin."

Emma nodded, Thomas fled to the kitchen and hauled out the biggest pot he could find, and Miriam dashed out to her cabin to snatch the prepacked midwifery bag she would need.

When she came back into the bedroom, she saw Emma leaning into Thomas and straining as a contraction hit. Miriam glanced at the clock and made a mental note.

"I'm going to prepare the bed," she said. "Stay on your feet as long as you feel comfortable."

With efficiency born of experience, Miriam stripped off the beautiful wedding quilt her other sister-in-law, Esther, had made for Thomas and Emma. Blankets and sheets followed. She placed a waterproof liner over the bare mattress, then remade the bed with clean sheets but no blankets. As she worked, another contraction hit, and her sister-in-law leaned into Thomas's arms to ride out the pain. Miriam nodded—two minutes apart.

"Come along, *liebling*, let's get you in bed." She glanced at her brother. "Would you mind giving us a couple minutes of privacy?"

"*Ja*, sure." Thomas looked pale. He gave his wife a quick kiss, then left the bedroom.

"Who's more nervous, you or him?" quipped Miriam as she settled Emma onto the bed.

"Oh, him, for sure and certain," replied Emma. Her smile turned to a grimace as another contraction came on.

Miriam examined the laboring woman, listened to the fetal heartbeat and came away pleased. "Everything's normal," she said. "Let me call Thomas back in." She opened the bedroom door and gestured at her brother.

"I'm guessing you'll be a father within an hour, probably less," she told him.

"I'm already a father," he replied. He sat next to the bed and let Emma grip his hands with crushing strength.

Miriam blinked back moisture. It was true. Her brother considered Hannah as much his daughter as the child Emma would soon bear.

Watching him murmur endearments to his wife, Miriam thought about Aaron. She had locked away that kiss, like a treasure in a box, in a secret part of her heart until she had the leisure to withdraw it and examine it more closely. Even more, she wanted more than just a kiss on the cheek. Would it one day be her, laboring to deliver a baby with Aaron by her side?

Emma alternately gritted her teeth and panted while

Thomas propped his wife up from behind. Miriam talked Emma through, encouraging her as her time grew closer.

A short while later, the baby was born. Emma's groans turned to shaky, tearful laughter.

"You have a boy!" exclaimed Miriam. "And he's beautiful."

"A son." Thomas didn't bother wiping away the tears coursing down his cheek. He dropped a kiss on the top of Emma's head. "A son, Emma!"

Miriam thanked *Gott* for the child's safe delivery. She cleaned up the baby and laid him across Emma's chest.

Tears trickled from the edges of the mother's eyes. "What a blessing it is to bear this child amid such love," Emma murmured.

Miriam knew Emma's disastrous first marriage had ended when she was widowed before Hannah was even born. She was pleased the woman's second marriage to Thomas was such a happy one.

Miriam bustled around the room, focusing on last-minute care while Emma and Thomas crooned over the baby.

"What name did you have in mind?" she finally asked.

Thomas looked up. "Jonathan," he said simply.

Miriam caught her breath. Their father's name had been Jonathan. He had died when Miriam was seventeen years old. "Oh, Thomas," she whispered.

Emma smiled over the baby's fuzzy, dark head. "*Gott ist gut*," she said.

"*Ja*, He is." Miriam blinked back her tears and packed up her midwifery bag. "I'm going to ask your uncle and aunt to keep Hannah overnight, if that's all right with you."

"*Ja, danke*," said Emma. "She's spent the night there many times, so they already have everything she'll need."

Miriam left her brother and sister-in-law to fuss over the new baby while she walked the short distance to the bishop's house.

"It's a boy," she announced with a smile when Lois Beiler answered her knock.

She gave a happy cry and clasped her hands to her chest. "Praise *Gott*!"

Little Hannah had been making cookies with her aunt. The child looked bewildered at the older woman's exclamation, so Miriam smiled at the girl. "You have a new baby *bruder*," she said.

"I do?" Hannah scrambled off the chair and flung herself at Miriam. "Can I see him?"

Miriam lifted the girl into her arms. "Your *mamm* asked if you could spend the night here," she said. "She just needs a little time to recover. *Ja?*"

"*Ja*, okay." Hannah bounced in Emma's arms. "A baby *bruder*! We can play games together!"

"I think it might be a little while before he's old enough to play games," Miriam cautioned as she put the child down. "But as soon as he's old enough, you can bet he'll want to play."

She turned to see the bishop standing in the doorway to his office, a huge grin on his face. "Another little one to spoil," the bishop said. Then, to Miriam's surprise, he said, "Would you mind coming into my office, Miriam? I wanted to talk to you."

Why would the church leader want to talk to her?

She glanced at Lois and saw encouragement in the older woman's face. "*Ja*, sure," she replied, and followed the bishop into his office. "Is something wrong?"

"*Nein*, not at all." The bishop gestured toward a chair as he dropped into his own seat. "But this is the second baby you've delivered since you came here to town. I wanted to ask if you've changed your mind about becoming a licensed midwife here in Montana and practicing your skills within the community."

Miriam clasped her hands. "I'm still working that through."

"Because you're so certain *Gott* hasn't forgiven you for losing a patient?"

"Ja..." She knew the time had come to admit her bargain. "Bishop, there's one thing you don't know. When I lost that patient, I made a promise to *Gott* that if He would forgive me, I would give Him my career, my training. I've already broken that promise, and it tears me up inside."

"Miriam, have you prayed for forgiveness?"

"Ja!" Tears sprang to her eyes. "Over and over again."

"Then it's done. Trying to bargain with *Gott* and promising him you'll give up your incredible skills in exchange for forgiveness isn't how *He* works. Forgiveness is a free gift."

Miriam knew that. Yet she had been so focused on sacrificing what was most valuable to her—her medical skills—that she'd never considered whether it was necessary or not. *Gott* had already offered a sacrifice on her behalf, on the cross. Her own sacrifice wasn't needed.

"Besides," the bishop continued, "you helped bring our new grand-nephew into the world a short time ago.

Do you think *Gott* would ask you to abandon someone in need by refusing to help?"

Miriam continued to clasp and unclasp her hands, trying to come to terms with what the bishop had said. Was she already forgiven? *Could* she continue practicing as a midwife?

"Now, let me ask you another question," he continued in the silence. "Do you *want* to give up medicine? Are you tired of practicing it? Or did you feel you *had* to give it up?"

"I don't want to give it up," she replied. "Especially the midwifery part. To me, that's the most rewarding aspect. When I watch the miracle of a new life coming into this world…"

"Then don't give it up," replied the bishop. A smile hovered on his lips. "We need someone with your skills here, Miriam. I would urge you to consider getting your license in Montana. You can restrict your midwifery to church members if that helps, rather than setting up your shingle in town. But I know every woman of childbearing age in Pierce would welcome you."

A great weight lifted off Miriam's shoulders. For one golden moment, she felt the utter sureness of *Gott*'s forgiveness—the forgiveness she had begged for—drift around her like a gilded cloud. Then it was gone, leaving behind a glow.

She lifted her head and looked into the older man's sympathetic eyes. "*Ja*," she replied. "I think I can do that."

"*Danke*," he replied simply.

Aaron found himself wondering if Miriam would make it back in time for his doctor's appointment. If not, he could always walk to town. He couldn't wait to get the cast off his arm so he could resume caring for his farm himself.

But he wanted to know how Emma was. Did the Kemps have a new son or a new daughter? He felt just a moment's envy. Like most Amish men, he'd looked forward to fatherhood. But now…

Major began bouncing along the fence line, making happy, gruffy noises. Aaron looked out the window and saw Miriam walking up the driveway. His heart leaped with gladness, and he, too, felt like bouncing along the fence line.

Instead, he stood on the front porch, waiting for her. Was it his imagination, or did she walk with a spring in her step? "What news?"

She grinned. "It's a boy."

He broke into a smile. "Praise *Gott*!"

"*Ja.* He's beautiful. And they named him Jonathan, after our father."

"*Ach*, that's wonderful."

Miriam climbed onto the porch and leaned against the balustrade. "And there's more. I had a short discussion with the bishop. He made me understand *Gott* had already forgiven me for losing that patient. Oh, Aaron, it was the most extraordinary feeling when I finally understood that, like a golden cloud enveloping me." Her face held an expression of wonder. "The bishop said I should strongly reconsider getting my Montana midwifery certification. And…and I think I will."

Gladness flowed through him. That would mean Miriam would stay. "That is *gut* news!"

"*Ja.* I don't plan to work in town, just here in the

Amish community. I may have to delay selling my car for a bit, too, since I'll have to sit for the state exam in Missoula. But I already have all the qualifications, so becoming certified should be a straightforward process."

"And you're happy about that," he observed.

She met his eyes. "*Ja*," she replied. "I'd been feeling adrift, unmoored, since making the decision to give up medicine. But this seems like the ideal compromise. I get to practice what I enjoy most—delivering babies—and it won't interfere with my goal of becoming baptized."

"If you want the truth, you look more at peace with yourself." She also looked dazzlingly beautiful in his eyes, but he knew better than to say that out loud.

"I *do* feel more peaceful. I hadn't realized what a burden it was, to feel unforgiven." Her face looked somber for a moment. "It was a heavy burden. But now..." Her face lit up, and she flung out her arms as if to embrace the porch, the sky, the dog...and him. "Now I feel light as air!"

He laughed.

Locking eyes with him, she dropped her arms. Her hazel eyes held a glow, a passion he hadn't seen since her arrival. "A lot of this is thanks to you," she said quietly. "You gave me the courage—both times—to deliver the babies."

"*N-nein*," he replied in a shaky voice. "*Gott* gave that to you. Never forget that, Miriam."

From inside the house, he heard the clock chime three times. Miriam gave a little start. "Your doctor's appointment!" she exclaimed. "It's in an hour, *ja*?"

"*Ja*. But I can walk there..."

"*Nein*, let me go hitch up your horse and buggy. I won't be long." She fled down the porch steps and dashed toward the barn.

Aaron watched her go, smiling. It didn't surprise him that she would insist on being there with him during the medical procedure. Miriam was a nurse through and through.

He quickly washed up and combed his hair while waiting for her to return. As he got ready, he realized something amazing: he wasn't worried about going to town. Yes, he knew he would be stared at, but somehow it seemed less important than before.

Within fifteen minutes, he heard the *clip-clop* of hooves and went out to meet Miriam, who was holding the reins with shy confidence.

"It's been years since I've driven a buggy," she told him. "But it's like riding a bicycle, ain't so? It all comes back."

He swung up into the seat next to her. "Maybe I can drive on the way home."

"Maybe." Clucking to the horse, they all took off down the gravel road.

Aaron looked around him as the Amish community gradually fell behind and the edge of town loomed ahead. "It's always a novelty to see this," he remarked. "I so seldom go to town."

She glanced at him. "Nervous?"

"*Ja*, but not for the reasons you think. I'm finding myself *oll recht* about being stared at. But I don't like hospitals, and I'm a little nervous about how they get the cast off."

"It's nothing. They'll use a cast saw to slice open the

cast, then it can be peeled off your arm. It's noisy, but the saw is very safe and won't harm the skin, even if it slips. I've done it lots of times. But trust me, you'll be relieved when it's off." She chuckled. "I could even use the saw and remove it for you, if they'd let me—but I doubt they will."

Aaron smiled. "You know, Miriam, even if you're limiting your Montana credentials to midwifery, having a qualified nurse in the community is a blessing."

Since the tiny town of Pierce didn't have enough space to accommodate Amish buggies on the primary road, Miriam guided the horse through a secondary road parallel to the main street. Within a few minutes, they'd pulled up to the hospital, and she hopped out and secured the horse to a hitching post. "I see the hospital is making adjustments for us," she noted, pointing at the hitching post.

"*Ja.* I've heard they've been very helpful." Aaron wiped one damp palm down his thigh. "Okay, let's get this over with."

Inside the building, he checked in with the receptionist. The young woman's eyes flickered to his scars, but she kept her voice professional and invited him to take a seat in the waiting room until they called his name.

After a short wait, a nurse called him back. Aaron was relieved when Miriam accompanied him.

"So how are you feeling?" the nurse asked as she examined the cast. She barely even glanced at his scars, to Aaron's relief.

"Absolutely fine, and ready to get back to work," he replied.

The woman flexed his fingers and seemed pleased.

"I'll remove the cast, and then the doctor will want to give you a final exam to make sure everything's healed properly."

The cast removal was as painless and noisy as Miriam had predicted, but when it was over, he felt the vast relief of having the heavy casing removed. "*Ach*, that's much better!" He lifted his arm experimentally.

The nurse smiled. "I'll be right back with the doctor."

The doctor came in a few moments later. "Ah, good afternoon, Mr. Lapp," he boomed cheerfully. "All healed up, I see. Let me take a look."

Aaron held out his arm, and the doctor probed it carefully. "Any pain here? Or here?" He tested the limb.

Aaron replied truthfully. "No. Everything's fine, and there's no pain."

"Then I see no reason for a follow-up visit, unless you experience any further complications." The doctor gave him some instructions for improving muscle tone, shook his hand and stepped out.

Aaron looked at Miriam with a smile of relief. "Let's go."

A few moments later, Miriam smiled at him as she unhitched the horse. "You see? No one said anything about your face," she teased. "Hopefully, you'll feel more comfortable coming to town on your own."

"Maybe." He leaned back against the buggy seat and gave a sigh of relief. "I'm glad that's over. I don't like hospitals."

"Or town?"

"Maybe."

"You'll be back in a couple weeks for Mountain Days," she reminded him.

"*Ja*, I will. I promised the bishop." *And you*, he added silently.

"It will be fine, Aaron. I'll be with you."

Aaron wondered if Miriam had any idea how much he craved that support.

Chapter Fifteen

In the two weeks before the Mountain Days Festival, Miriam divided her time between Aaron's farm and cooing over her newborn nephew.

"You're a *gut* big sister," she told Hannah one morning. The child was in love with her infant brother, and Miriam walked in to see the baby lying on a blanket on the floor, surrounded by a selection of Hannah's toys. "The *boppli* is too little to play with anything yet, but I'm sure he likes seeing everything you put here."

Emma chuckled at her little daughter's enthusiasm. "She's a sweet girl."

"Ja." Miriam picked Hannah up and twirled her around, making the girl shriek with laughter. She knew it was important to give love and attention to an older child when a new baby arrived. "I was going to make cookies this afternoon in my cabin. Do you want to help?"

"Ja, bitte!"

"It will give your *mamm* a chance to take a nap too. And you can help me plan next year's garden." It was a game she had devised with her niece—to sketch out a future garden and plant make-believe vegetables. Emma's gardening skills were being handed down to her daughter, who loved to draw pretend gardens full of herbs and vegetables.

Miriam put Hannah back down. "I'm going to go help milk Aaron's cows. We can make the cookies this afternoon, *oll recht*?" She looked at Emma. "You're looking *gut*."

"Danke." Emma patted her belly. "I'll be glad to lose this, though."

"You're still the most beautiful woman Thomas ever saw. He told me that just yesterday."

Emma blushed. "I'm glad he thinks so."

Miriam gave Hannah a kiss on the cheek. "I'm off to milk the cows. I'll be back in a few hours."

The morning was cloudy and promised rain later in the day. Miriam could smell the change in the air, both with the impending rain and with the change of seasons. For the first time, she detected an early hint of autumn.

As was her habit, she went through the kitchen door to pick up the sterilized buckets but found them missing. Which meant Aaron was already in the barn, milking.

Major came bouncing out to meet her as she walked toward the outbuilding. She patted the huge animal, who lumbered by her side as she approached the barn.

Sure enough, Aaron sat on the milking crate before Matilda, his favorite cow. But the animal wasn't in the milking stall, and Aaron wasn't milking—at least, not with his hands. Instead, he was holding the prototype of the milking device he had been working on.

"Look at this!" he said, his voice rising with enthusiasm. "It's working!"

She peered over his shoulder. "How does it work?" she asked.

"All I do is pump this handle once or twice," he replied. "It creates a vacuum that draws out the milk, right into the bottle. In some ways, it's better than milking into an open bucket since the milk stays perfectly clean. Matilda doesn't seem to mind it either. It's a little slower than hand-milking because I'm only milking one quarter at a time, but it's easier. Lots easier."

"Aaron, that's amazing." She was deeply impressed at the cleverness of the machine. "I can see lots of people wanting this."

"*Ja*, that's my hope." He gave the handle a single pump, and milk flowed into the bottle with renewed strength.

"I wonder..." Miriam watched the amazing little device and marveled anew at Aaron's creative mind. "I wonder if you could come up with a version that could milk two quarters at a time. That would make it just about as efficient as hand-milking, wouldn't it?"

There was a moment's silence; then Aaron turned to look at her, a smile on his face. "*Ja*!" he said. "I've been so focused on just this one prototype, it never occurred to me. But making a two-quarter milker modeled on the same principle wouldn't be hard. I could have the rubber cups attached to hoses that lead into the chamber..."

She could almost see the gears churning in his brain as he mentally designed the idea, and she smiled at his enthusiasm. "How many cows have you milked?" she asked.

"Just Matilda," he said, almost apologetic.

"No worries. I'll get the others going. Come along,

Bossy, you're first." She opened the gate to the milking stall, and the small herd's matriarch immediately moved inside.

"I'm going to start building my festival booth today," Aaron remarked behind her as she started zinging warm milk into the waiting bucket. "I could use your help with it."

"Well, I'm not much *gut* at swinging a hammer," she warned.

"Not for the building of it—more in the design aspect. I've talked to Benjamin Troyer. He's the one in charge of organizing the church participation in the event. He's given me some ideas, but frankly, I think the booth will need a woman's touch when it comes to the layout."

"*Ja*, sure." Miriam pressed her forehead into the cow's warm flank, glad for any excuse to remain in Aaron's company. She had stopped coming to his farm in the afternoon since he could do the barn chores himself now, and she found herself missing seeing him twice a day. "I did promise Hannah I'd make cookies with her this afternoon—more as an excuse to give Emma time for a nap than anything else, but I told her it would be in the afternoon."

"It won't take long to sketch out. It's more than just the construction I'd like your input on—it's also how to make the booth eye-catching and interesting. Benjamin suggested things like bunting and signage. I'm not quite sure what to do with it."

"I can sew the bunting. Just let me know the colors you want and where you want the fabrics."

"*Danke!* That would be great." He chuckled. "I was

hesitant to ask, because I wasn't sure about your sewing skills."

"I'm not an expert seamstress, but I can get by. Certainly bunting and some swagging shouldn't be a problem. How many inventions do you plan to showcase?"

Aaron rubbed his chin. "I have about ten, I figure. I hope to have a few duplicates I can sell, such as the chicken feeders, but mostly it's just going to be information only."

Miriam didn't mention the most obvious aspect of an information booth: that it would mean talking about his inventions to a wide variety of people. It would be a truly monumental step in Aaron's recovery if he could make it through the entire day talking with *Englisch* strangers, facing their stares unflinchingly and acting as though he had never been hiding in isolation. She knew it would take a lot out of him, and she was glad she was going to be there to help him through the ordeal.

"Emma is hoping to send a bunch of soap to sell," she said as she finished milking Bossy and allowed the animal to back out of the pen. She released the cow and snapped a lead rope on the halter of the next one. "Would it be possible to make a sort of divided booth? You can man one side with your inventions, I can sell Emma's soaps on the other?"

"*Ja*, sure. That would be easy. She already has display cases built, doesn't she?"

"*Ja*, Thomas made some for her. Most are in the store, but she has a few smaller ones I could use in the booth."

"When we're finished up in here, let's go sketch it out."

Miriam liked how Aaron used the term *let's*. It implied a togetherness she enjoyed and looked forward to every day. Now that he had the cast off, he was doing far more work around the farm and regaining strength in his injured arm. She liked to think he was regaining emotional strength as well.

Aaron was smiling more and more lately. It was unforced and casual, and seemed *un*-self-conscious. She found herself smiling back; she was falling in love with him.

This presented a quandary. Half an hour later, bent over a sheet of paper on the kitchen table, making suggestions while he sketched out what he hoped the booth would look like, she wondered if she should reveal her feelings to him.

No. Some inner voice told her it was too early in Aaron's recovery to throw such a bomb at him. But she also recognized the certainty of them. There was so much to admire about the man: his efficiency around the farm, his determination to be self-sufficient, his clever and creative mind, his love for his animals, the strength he offered her while she dealt with her own raw emotions from her past. She knew Aaron was the man for her.

As she sat there at the table with him, she had a vision of what a future with Aaron would be like. Building up the farm, helping him with his inventions, having dinner with her brother and sister-in-law across the road, welcoming children…

It was a comforting, golden vision.

She only hoped it was a vision Aaron shared. If not… well, then her future would be very different.

Aaron began construction of his booth after Miriam left. When he had first bought this farm after leaving

Pennsylvania, the property had several rotting outbuildings he had torn down. But he had carefully saved the lumber, knowing it might come in handy. He used some of that lumber now to build the booth.

It had started to rain, so he worked in the barn. The air was warm despite the precipitation, and he wiped sweat from his face and neck with a handkerchief as he worked. His plan was to make the structure in pieces that could be easily assembled and disassembled, with components small enough to be transported in his wagon.

It felt good to work again, unhampered by the heavy cast. His arm was not as strong as it had been, but that strength would return as long as he continued to work it.

Banging nails and sawing lumber occupied his body, but it left his mind free. And his mind dwelled, as it so often did, on Miriam.

More than anything, he wanted to court her. These last few weeks had demonstrated that she never flinched from his company. In fact, she seemed to welcome it… or at least, he hoped she did.

But when her sister-in-law had gone into labor and he had kissed her to break the panic…that had cemented it for him. The kiss had been nothing more than a means to an end, a method to snap her out of her anxiety, but the very fact that she hadn't pulled away in disgust gave him hope.

Aaron paused and looked around the barn. The large structure was divided into areas for different purposes: A workshop. Hay storage. Feed boxes for the cattle. Pens for the calves. The milking parlor. Indoor shelter for the cows when the weather was inclement. Horse stalls. And it was all his. Thanks to the hard work he'd put in saving for a farm in expensive Pennsylvania when he was courting Denise, he had been able to pay full price for this land in Montana since the cost was so much lower. Now he owned the farm outright but had no woman to share it with.

He hammered and measured and sawed, lost in a dream of what it would be like to have Miriam in his life on a daily basis—and not just in the barn. In the house. Around the fields. By the pond. Sharing the work, sharing the laughter, sharing the livestock…sharing their lives.

Suddenly he missed a nail and smacked his thumb instead. "Ouch!" Angry at himself, he waved the injured digit and jumped around in pain.

The slight mishap jerked him out of his imaginary future and back to reality. It was time to stop daydreaming and focus on the task at hand. A future with Miriam was by no means assured, no matter how much he wanted it.

He paused for a moment to count his blessings. For one, there was his health. His broken arm was mended, the accident had not deprived him of his vision or hearing, and he was young and strong. For another, there was his farm. *Gott* had provided him with a refuge in his time of need, and this farm represented the sanctuary, a place to lick his wounds and nurse the blows he'd received. For a third, there was the church community. They had welcomed him, giving him both the privacy he craved as well as the spiritual support he required.

Now, to his astonishment, he realized his position in the community had shifted. He seemed more a part of it now. The Kemps had welcomed him as both a friend and a neighbor. The bishop had requested his participation in the Mountain Days event. He talked more easily with the other men after church services.

Maybe it was more than his broken arm that had healed. If so, he knew he owed it to Miriam. Whether or not she would ever welcome his courtship, he owed her a debt of gratitude.

Unquestionably, he considered Miriam the greatest blessing. Her company, her acceptance of his appearance, her laughter, her no-nonsense approach to life—what a woman.

One thing was certain: she had taught him to smile again. For that reason, even if he had no hope she would ever welcome his courtship, he would show her his smile, not his pain.

Resuming his work, he could feel his thumb throb. In fact, his healed arm was a bit shaky. Maybe it was time to stop the carpentry for the moment—no sense overdoing it so soon after having the cast removed.

What he really wanted was an excuse to walk across the road and see Miriam. She mentioned she was going to make cookies with Hannah. He brushed some sawdust off the front of his shirt, placed his straw hat on his head, gave Major an affectionate scratch and set off toward Miriam's cabin.

The rain pattered lightly on his hat. Aaron bypassed the main house and walked toward the back, where Miriam's cabin was located.

The door was open, and he could hear voices inside.

"That one looks like it will need a raisin for the nose, don't you think?" he heard Miriam say.

"Like this?" Hannah's higher-pitched voice sounded like a younger version of her mother's.

"*Ja.* Now it makes a proper gingerbread man, ain't so?"

Aaron knocked on the door frame. "Anyone home?"

"Aaron!" Miriam smiled at him, smudges of flour on her apron. "I didn't expect to see you."

Her slight dishabille looked beautiful to him. "I was working on the booth and managed to smack my thumb." He held up the offended digit. "Plus, my arm muscles were getting a little shaky, and I decided it was wiser not to overdo it. Instead, I had a couple questions about the bunting for the booth."

She cocked an eyebrow at him, and her eyes twinkled. "Is that the *only* reason you're here?"

"Just wanted to see you," he confessed, his heart beating fast.

The half-smile on her face weakened his knees. "Well, you're just in time for some warm gingerbread cookies." Miriam looked at Hannah. "Which one should we give him, do you think?"

"Hmm. How about this one?" The child pointed.

"*Ja, gut* choice." Miriam used a spatula to slide the treat onto a small plate, which she handed to Aaron. "Have a seat."

He squeezed into a chair lodged under the window by the small kitchen table and nibbled the cookie.

"Did you really have a question about the bunting?" she asked, rolling out dough with efficient movements.

"Not really. I mean, there's plenty of time to figure out the details. This is very *gut*," he added.

"*Danke*. I had lots of help." She kissed Hannah on her head.

The domestic sweetness of the scene—the warm cookies, the delectable smells, an eager child helping, even the soft rain outside—gave Aaron a sharp stab of longing. His home always seemed more complete when Miriam was inside it. He wondered what it would take to have her there always. He wondered what it would be like to have a child like Hannah, someone who would look upon his ravaged features with love…

"Why the long face?" Miriam asked him gently.

He blinked back to reality. "*Ach*, just enjoying the picture this makes," he said honestly, gesturing toward the whole cabin and including the child and the messy table. Then he added daringly, "Sometimes a bachelor gets tired of staring at the same four walls all the time."

"Now, that's a change." Miriam gave Hannah a cookie cutter and let the child press shapes into the dough. "I seem to remember a time you wanted nothing but solitude."

"Things *have* changed," he admitted.

She looked at him, and he tried not to read deeper meaning in the soft depths of her hazel eyes. "You're always *welkom* here, Aaron," she said gently.

He sincerely hoped she meant it…because he intended to take her up on it.

Chapter Sixteen

Aaron slid the last of the side panels for his booth into the back of the wagon. The booth had turned out better than he'd hoped, and yesterday he'd shown Miriam how easy it was to assemble and then break down the temporary structure. "Just a few screws, and it's solid as a rock," he said, demonstrating his method.

Now the big morning was here—the Mountain Days Festival, where he would be exposing himself to the gazes of *Englisch* strangers all day long. *Just smile all the time*, Miriam had suggested, and he intended to follow her advice.

He rose before dawn to milk the cows, then finished packing the wagon, including the colorful bunting Miriam had sewn for him. He carefully placed the prototype for his milker in a crate. He also packed multiple examples of his other farm inventions in case someone was interested in purchasing one. He had made some signage for everything, explaining each device's purpose. Then he loaded two stools so he and Miriam could sit down. He had thought through every possible contingency of what he might need throughout the day and made sure he had it with him.

"You have to stay here, buddy," he told Major as the giant Newfoundland hung around the wagon, seeming to know something was up.

When everything was ready, Aaron swung into the wagon seat, clucked to the horse, and drove down the driveway, across the road, and up to Thomas and Emma's house.

"*Guder mariye*," called out Thomas, coming outside with a box in his arms. "Are you ready for the day?"

"*Ja*, I think so." Aaron smiled at his neighbor. "I left room for plenty of soap, so hopefully Miriam will be able to sell a lot."

Thomas loaded the box into the wagon as Emma emerged from the house with her infant son in her arms. "*Guder mariye*, Aaron," she said. "*Vielen dank* for letting Miriam sell some soap for me."

"Not a problem. Miriam said you had signs for each soap, *ja*?"

"*Ja*, with prices and everything."

"And here are the display cases." Thomas lifted some lightweight wooden boxes built on angles to display the variety of soaps. "Each one has a label so Miriam can load them correctly."

It took a few minutes to get all the products loaded. As they settled the last of the soap into the wagon, Miriam came hurrying around from the back of the house, shoving a pin into her hair to secure her *kapp*. "Sorry. I almost overslept," she apologized.

Aaron thought she had never looked more beautiful. "You're not late," he told her.

Miriam hugged her brother and sister-in-law. "I don't know when I'll be back, but likely late afternoon." Then she climbed onto the wagon seat as Aaron lifted the reins and directed the horse down the driveway.

The morning was fresh and sparkling clear. A wide variety of wagons joined them on the gravel road toward town as members of the church community made their way with a common goal: to demonstrate and showcase their skills, talents and products at the town celebration. There were calls of greeting back and forth among the vehicles.

In past years, Aaron had always been a spectator. Now he was part of it—and found himself happy to be so.

"Nervous?" Miriam inquired as she waved to the occupants of another wagon.

"A bit," he replied. "But surprisingly, I'm looking forward to it. It will certainly be a test."

"In some ways, the biggest one you've faced yet." She patted his shoulder. "You're strong, Aaron. Never forget that."

Aaron wondered if she had any idea how much of his strength came from her.

The area set aside for the Amish demonstration was generous in size and included a cordoned-off area with trees, where the horses could be let loose for the day. Aaron saw a large number of booths being set up for demonstrating a wide variety of skills: leatherworking, basket-weaving, butter-churning, even pie-making. One farmer had brought in several of his Jersey milk cows and set up stools and buckets to show interested visitors how to milk. Two farmers had brought their draft horses and plowing equipment, ready to demonstrate horse-powered agriculture in a designated field. Several quilting frames were being set up under the shade of some canopies.

"Wow," he said. "This is impressive."

"*Ja*, it is." Miriam gazed around, her eyes bright with interest. "This is just as new to me as it is to you."

Following the direction of Benjamin Troyer, Aaron offloaded the wagon, then went to park and unhitch the horse. There was a carnival atmosphere among the church members. He heard laughter, jokes, and the sound of hammers as people set up their displays and booths.

"*Guder mariye*," several people hailed him. "So *gut* to see you here!"

He was warmed by their enthusiasm.

It didn't take long to get his own booth built with Miriam's help. "You're right," she commented as the structure took shape. "It's easy to set up."

They hung the colorful bunting, set up Emma's soap display and carefully arranged Aaron's collection of inventions, along with signage explaining their purpose. Finally, they hung a sign requesting no photography—a request from the bishop for every booth, which most church members knew would likely be ignored by *Englisch* visitors.

"Let the hurricane roar," he commented as he and Miriam completed the setup.

"Just in time too. Look." Miriam pointed toward some early visitors strolling through.

Within an hour, the Amish-demonstration area was busy. "Just smile," Miriam whispered as their first visitors ambled over.

Aaron tried not to grit his teeth as the older couple

each did a double take when seeing his ravaged face, but he did as Miriam suggested and smiled broadly. To his surprise, it worked. The couple instantly relaxed and asked him about what he had on display, and he pointed out his farm inventions. The woman sniffed the soaps and purchased two bars; then they went on their way.

He let out a loud sigh of relief. "Okay, that went better than I'd hoped."

"The vast majority of people are nice," she said. "You did great, Aaron. Keep it up."

Her words proved prophetic. The crowds grew thick, and Aaron kept a smile plastered on his face. A few children stared, but the adults—after a quick shocked look—invariably turned out to be polite and interested.

In the early afternoon, an older man with a neatly trimmed beard and cowboy hat wandered by. He barely glanced at Aaron's scars; instead, he carefully read the signage, then picked up the milking device and looked it over.

"So this milks cows?" he inquired.

"*Ja*," replied Aaron. He took the prototype and explained how it worked.

"I see." The man took the device in his hands and examined it. "Where have you marketed this?"

"I haven't," Aaron replied, startled. "I was just going to make a few of them for older church members. After all, how many people outside our own community milk their own cows?"

"You'd be surprised." The man offered him a business card. "My name is Buck Winston. I have a small manufacturing company that specializes in agricultural products. I'm very interested in this device and would like to consider its commercial applications. Are you interested?"

Aaron stuttered for a moment before recovering. "*J-ja*, sure," he said. "I never thought it might have a commercial application. I just like coming up with things to help our church members." He gestured toward the rest of his inventions.

Buck Winston looked carefully over the other items, then nodded. "These are all cleverly made, but the milker has the most potential. Is there a phone number where I can reach you?"

"*Nein*. In our church, we don't use telephones. But I can give you my address, and you're welcome to come by in person to discuss it further." Aaron took a slip of paper and wrote his address on it, then handed it to the man.

"Thank you." He shook Aaron's hand. "I'll be in touch. I think you might be pleasantly surprised by what I can do for you."

In a mild state of shock, Aaron watched until the man was lost in the crowd of people, then he turned to Miriam. "What just happened?"

Spontaneously, she threw her arms around him and gave him a hug. "It means your invention might make a profit! Oh, Aaron, I'm so proud of you!"

Never in his life had Aaron been happier than at that moment, when he hugged her back.

Aaron's arms tightened around her waist, and time stood still.

Miriam stood motionless, hardly daring to breathe. She caught her breath, staring into his dark blue eyes,

eyes that looked darker than normal. The sounds of the festival, the ebb and flow of people around them, faded into an indistinct buzz. The only thing she saw was Aaron.

"Miriam," he breathed, and she saw a plea in his eyes.

She lowered her arms. He released her waist. But she still stared, aware something very important was happening between them.

"Everything *oll recht*?"

Miriam jumped back. So did Aaron. Benjamin Troyer stood at the front of the booth, watching them with an inquiring look on his face.

Miriam felt herself blush. She knew very well Benjamin had witnessed the impulsive hug. She hoped he was unaware of the earth-shattering realization behind it.

"*J-ja*," stuttered Aaron. "I just had a man come by who made me an incredible offer."

"I'm just making the rounds and checking on all the booths," Benjamin said. He hefted a sign that had slipped off the front of the structure. "This fell off, by the way. What kind of offer?"

"He wants to look into commercial manufacturing for my milking device." Aaron gestured toward the prototype.

Miriam was amazed he was able to act as nonchalant as he was, while she herself was still breathless.

Benjamin broke into a smile. "Aaron, that's wonderful!" He reached out to shake hands.

Aaron laughed a bit as he accepted the gesture.

"*Danke.* I'm a little dazed. I honestly never thought this had any potential beyond our own church community."

"My advice is to bring in a lawyer to help with any discussions," suggested Benjamin. "You might be able to negotiate something like a percentage of any unit sold or something like that. It could net you a nice income if the device takes off."

"*Ja, gut* idea." Aaron removed his hat, ran a hand through his hair and replaced the head covering. "I'm still in shock."

"I can imagine. Do you need any help replacing this sign?" Benjamin pointed to the wood piece.

"*Nein*, I can handle it." Aaron stepped out of the booth and squatted in front, rehanging the sign from where it had fallen off its hooks.

Benjamin stepped toward Miriam's side of the booth. "How are Emma's soaps selling?" he inquired.

"Very well," she replied. "I can see why she thought she had the potential to open her own storefront last year. I never realized how much people enjoyed scented bars..."

Then disaster struck.

A small boy, perhaps four years old, ran past, laughing. His foot caught on the grass, and he tripped and fell. Instinctively, Aaron rose from where he had finished rehanging the sign and went to assist the child. "Whoa, little man. Are you hurt?" He helped the boy to his feet.

The child looked up at Aaron and let out a scream.

Miriam sucked in her breath.

Aaron dropped the boy's arm, and she saw a look of such pitiful withdrawal on his face that her heart broke.

The situation was exacerbated when a woman, presumably the child's mother, ran up and snatched the boy away from Aaron. Her face was suffused with horror as she stared at him. "Leave my child alone!" she shrilled, backing up with the weeping boy in her arms.

People stopped what they were doing. They stared. They whispered. They pointed.

Aaron drew himself up, raised his chin and stood stock-still.

Then Benjamin stepped forward. "Your son fell, ma'am, and this man merely helped him to his feet," he explained.

"I don't care. Leave us alone." The woman's voice was strident. She turned and disappeared into the crowd.

And then Aaron turned and walked away too. In disbelief, Miriam watched as he simply walked away from the demonstration area and vanished from sight.

She heard Benjamin mutter some uncharitable words directed at the woman and her child under his breath before turning a sympathetic face toward Miriam. "I'm sorry. What a setback," he observed.

She felt moisture spring to her eyes. "*Ja.* He was doing so well too—smiling all day long and talking to people."

"Well, give him a few minutes to cool down. I expect he'll be fine."

"No doubt. I'm glad you were here as a witness, Benjamin. Sometimes the *Englischer* can do some foolish things. I hope she doesn't try to sue or something like that."

"Let's hope not. I'll check back in a little while to see how he's doing."

Benjamin moved away, continuing his rounds in the Amish section of the festival, and Miriam strained to see where Aaron might have gone.

But he didn't come back.

Chapter Seventeen

Aaron walked all the way home, feeling stunned.

All his hard-won confidence was gone. He felt demoralized, depressed. All it took was one child to react, and he felt himself transformed into the monster the boy probably saw him as.

He recalled the stark terror in the child's eyes, the loathing on the face of his mother as she snatched her son in her arms and backed up. He couldn't have done a more thorough job if he'd worn a scary mask and shouted, "Boo!"

Dimly, he knew he shouldn't have left Miriam in the booth alone, but he couldn't bear the thought of remaining in town, the object of whispers and stares from terrified little children.

It took him an hour to reach his farm. He saw no one during the walk. Everyone was either staying home that day or already at the Mountain Days Festival. As he walked up his driveway, Major loped toward the gate, his canine face smiling and his tail wagging. Aaron sank down on the porch steps and simply hugged the dog.

Major had never let him down. His animals were the one dependable staple in his life, the creatures who accepted him for who he was.

He saw again the child's terrified face as he screamed. Would that always happen? Would he always be the recipient of fear and recoil?

"Why, *Gott*, why?" he cried, startling the dog. He buried his head in Major's fur, and then the tears came.

He wept for his lost face, for the affliction that was so severe that it frightened young children and their mothers.

As he wept, he made a bitter resolve: Never again would he darken the town. Never again would he leave his farm unless he had to. He would go to church—despite his anger, he could never abandon *Gott*—and he would participate when requested by church members to help with community projects, but that was it.

The rest of the time, he would stay here, with his animals, doing whatever it took to make a living by the fruits of his labor. He had planned it that way since moving to Montana; now he would continue.

He was alone. He would stay alone. Instead of haunting an opera house like the disfigured character from the novel, he would haunt his farm and stay where he would never be mocked or tormented. He was like a beast, crawling into his lair to lick his wounds.

He hugged the dog harder. The animal, as if sensing he was needed, stayed calm and passive in the embrace.

At last, Aaron lifted his face from the dog's fur and groped for a handkerchief to wipe his tears.

The initial shame and anguish passed, and in a way, he felt better. The encounter in town simply reminded him to turn back to the lifestyle he had chosen anyway—solitude. He was right to stay on his farm and not scare others. He heaved a great shuddering sigh and stood up. "*Danke*, my friend," he told Major, tousling the fur around the dog's ears.

He went into the house. The interior was neat and tidy now, thanks to Miriam's example. Aaron looked around and counted his blessings. He had his wall of books that gave him great comfort and company on winter evenings. He had the kitchen, equipped to handle the projects he had taught himself—canning and cheese-making and butter-making. He had the garden to provide for his needs. He had a massive supply of firewood, neatly stacked in the woodshed. He had the pantry and root cellar, for storing what he made or grew. He had the barn, for housing the animals that provided his livelihood. He had the chickens, for meat and eggs.

Yes, he had much to be grateful for. *Gott* had deprived him of his looks but provided for his needs.

It was too early for barn chores, but he went out to the barn anyway. The cats wound around his ankles, purring affectionately. The cows were out in their pasture. Some grazed; others lay chewing their cud, the picture of utter contentment. In the coop, the chickens clucked and scratched on the compost mound; the rooster crowed and stayed vigilant over his flock.

All this was his. He owned it all. It was completely paid for, and he owed no one a dime, except for whatever yearly expenses he incurred.

Yes, *Gott* had provided for him. He should never have attempted to thwart *Gott*'s will by showing his face in town. He wouldn't make that mistake again.

He stood in the doorway of the barn, looking out at the fields and the woods of his domain, and finally got up the courage to take the hidden shining jewel from the pocket of his heart and examine it. Miriam.

Had he imagined the emotion when she'd hugged him? Was he pinning hopes on her where none existed? Was he misplacing his own desperate yearning for a wife on a woman who was simply being friendly and supportive?

Where did Miriam fit into this future life of solitude he had planned?

She didn't. Solitude was, by definition, not shared with anyone else. He was grateful to her for the endless things she had done for him since the night he broke his arm—but he wouldn't risk the heartbreak of having her reject any romantic interests simply because he misinterpreted friendliness for something else.

Above all, he would never ask another person to share a life of solitude. It simply wasn't fair. If *Gott* wanted him to be alone, he would stay alone.

There was an old saying from a famous poet about how much better it was to have loved and lost than to never have loved at all. Was that the case for him? Having fallen in love with Miriam, he now must steel himself to lose her. He would not burden her with a man whose face terrified little children.

He didn't think he had imagined that spark in her eyes when she'd embraced him. But even if it was real, how could he yoke himself with her and chain her to a monster? No. It was better to let her go, let her be courted by a handsome man who wasn't ashamed to be seen in town, someone who would provide her with children as pretty as herself. Her beauty didn't need his beast.

He ran a hand over his face—at first, in a gesture of despair, then in a moment of exploration. The thick scars merely confirmed his decision. Major walked up beside him and leaned on his leg, as if offering comfort. Aaron dropped his hand to his dog, stroking the animal's massive head. This was all he needed. His dog.

By the afternoon, his guilt started up. He'd left Miriam to deal with the booth alone, not to mention the horse and wagon. He thought briefly about walking back to help pack everything up, but he was too ashamed to consider it.

He had a feeling Miriam would give him a much-deserved tongue-lashing when she returned—and frankly, he knew he deserved anything she dumped on him.

At long last, he began to hear the familiar *clip-clop* of hooves as church members returned from the festival. From his position in the barn, he could just glimpse through the trees to the vehicles passing on the gravel road. Ephraim King drove at walking speed, with three Jersey cows tied to the back of his wagon. Eli Miller also drove his wagon, drawn by plow horses and with the plow loaded onto the wagon. Others drove buggies packed with their own demo items.

And then there was Miriam, guiding the horse up the driveway with the wagon full of booth components. She stopped in front of the gate, dismounted from the wagon to open it, led the horse through closed the gate behind her, then climbed back up on the wagon seat. From this distance, he couldn't see the expression on her face, but from her stiff posture he could guess her emotions. He braced himself to take whatever she dealt out, because he deserved every bit of it.

He straightened his shoulders and went to meet her at the front of the barn, where the horse was normally unhitched.

When Miriam saw how Aaron had responded to the woman and her child—his dignity in the face of fear and rejection—in that moment, she knew she loved him deeply. She had loved him for some time, but this reinforced it.

He had stood straight and tall, emotionless, his shoulders back and his chin raised, and had said nothing.

Then he'd walked away without a word. She expected—as Benjamin had suggested—that he simply went off to cool down a bit. But as the hours ticked by and the festival wound down, it became clear he wasn't coming back. He had simply abandoned her and the booth.

Benjamin came by as the event was drawing to a close. "Aaron didn't come back?" he asked in surprise.

Miriam kept her temper under control. "No."

"I see." He rubbed his chin. "I'll help you break down the booth."

"*Danke.* I would be grateful."

It had taken an hour to pack away the soaps and inventions, and disassemble the booth. At least Miriam knew how to easily take it apart—Aaron, in his enthusiasm, had made sure of that. Benjamin took it upon himself to hitch up the horse, then helped Miriam load everything into the wagon.

When all was finished, she thanked Benjamin. "*Vielen dank.* I could have done this myself, but it would have taken a lot longer."

"*Bitte.*" Benjamin looked troubled. "I hope Aaron comes out of this okay. Let me know if I can do anything."

Miriam thinned her lips. "I have a few words to say to him, I can assure you."

She thought she saw a spark of humor in the man's eyes, but he merely nodded his head and said his goodbyes.

Miriam directed the horse homeward. She drove with eyebrows furrowed and lips compressed. Yes, she had a few words to say to Aaron, all right. What she had to say would either make or break any future they might have together.

She saw Aaron waiting for her in front of the barn, where he normally hitched and unhitched the wagon or buggy.

She drew up in front of him and pulled the horse to a stop. Aaron wore an expression that was both remorseful and defiant.

"Are you done sulking?" she asked coldly.

He lifted his chin, and his eyes cooled. "I wasn't sulking."

"Could've fooled me." She climbed down from the wagon. "Meet me in the house when you're finished unhitching. I want to talk to you." Without a backward glance, she marched toward the house and let herself in. Major danced at her heels, glad to see her. But she merely gave the dog a cursory pat, and the aggrieved animal went to his bed and curled up with a huffy sigh.

She paced the living room, her skirts swishing in her agitation, trying to gather her thoughts into something coherent. She *had* to find some way to penetrate Aaron's self-imposed victimhood.

He came in a few minutes later, wearing the same defiant expression. "Miriam, I'm sorry I left you to finish out the day like that—"

She whirled around. "You should be. What you did was inexcusable. But it's more than that."

"*What*'s more?"

"Your attitude. I'm tired of catering to your demons, Aaron. I won't have it."

His face went grim, an expression that emphasized the scars. "You won't have to. I had a good long time to think this afternoon, and I realize it was a mistake to show myself in public. *Gott* wants me to stay here on the farm. I know that now."

"Is that so?" She crossed her arms and glared at him. "What makes you so sure?"

"You saw what happened. I scared an *Englisch* child. He looked at me like I was a monster. His mother snatched him away because she saw a monster too. Do you think that's the kind of thing I want to have happen every time I go to town?"

"One kid overreacts, and you're resigning yourself to a life of solitude?" she asked furiously. "You're letting one little setback affect your confidence. That's cowardly, Aaron."

"If I'm a coward, so are you."

She stared at him for a moment. "What are you talking about?"

"You had the same thing happen," he growled. "You

lost a patient through no fault of your own. For that, you were willing to throw away years of medical training. Now who's the coward?"

In the sudden silence, she heard the clock tick loudly. Miriam realized he was right. She *had* been willing to throw away years of medical training over the first patient she'd lost.

"If that's the case," she said more quietly, "I got over the trauma, thanks in part to you. Now, what are you doing to get over *your* trauma?"

"I can't." He turned away. "No amount of counseling or surgery or even prayer will take away these scars. I'm a beast, and a beast I'll remain, regardless of how the fairy tale ends. That's why it's best to just stay here on the farm."

"For the rest of your life?"

"*Ja.* For the rest of my life.

She glared. "I've overcome my self-doubt enough to start my career again. Will you ever do the same? It's your attitude that's chasing people away, Aaron, not your scars."

"Except when it comes to children and their mothers." He glared back.

"You're still catering to your demons. It's time you either face them or succumb to them. If it's the latter, I'm through with you."

She saw him almost visibly withdraw into himself. "It's no less than I expected," he said harshly. "It's happened before. That's why I've decided it's easier to be alone." He turned away and faced his wall of books, the books he'd admitted sustained him through his solitude.

Her anger left her. He honestly seemed to believe

what he said. How could she penetrate his shield? She quieted her voice. "For the rest of your life, people will stare at first—and occasionally, a child may be frightened. That's reality. You're going to have to accept it. But once they get to know you, they'll see the vibrant, compelling man underneath and grow to like you for who you truly are."

"Like you?" He spoke quietly, still facing his books.

"*Ja*," she said softly. "Like me."

The clock could be heard again, ticking in the silence.

Aaron turned to look at her, and she saw a spark in his eyes. "What are you saying?"

She gave him a sad smile. "Haven't you noticed? I've enjoyed your company from the start, Aaron, but it's ripened into something more. At least, on my part."

He stared for a moment as if he didn't believe her. His voice was harsh. "You're a beautiful woman, Miriam. You could have any man you want. Why would you want a misshapen monster?"

"Because I don't see a monster. I see a fascinating man who helped me heal my own trauma. Why can't you accept that you're still the same person underneath?" The smile fell away. "But I refuse to proceed with a courtship if you can't or won't address your own fears."

The expression on his face—a mixture of wild hope and trembling joy—highlighted the handsome man he had once been. "Courtship?"

"You heard me. But you're going to have to meet me halfway—" she pointed to a spot on the floor "—as an agreement to face the future. A future that includes going off the farm."

Major changed position on his dog bed and emitted a huge sigh. In the distance, a rooster crowed.

Aaron took a step forward.

Miriam took a step forward.

He snaked his arms around her waist. She looped her arms around his neck.

"Are you serious?" he murmured.

For her answer, she kissed him, giving in to the emotions she had felt for weeks.

At last, Aaron pressed his forehead to hers. "I love you," he whispered. "I've loved you almost from the start. But I had convinced myself beauty could never love the beast."

A wave of overwhelming love for the man in her arms washed over her. "You're not a beast, Aaron. Inside, you're beautiful. The most beautiful man I've ever met. I've been in love with you for some time, but you weren't ready to hear it. Are you now?"

"*Ja*," he choked out. "I am now. Will you let me court you?"

She laughed through her tears. "I'd say you're courting me right now, don't you think?"

He dipped his head for another kiss. Then he broke it off to embrace her fiercely. Miriam felt the pounding of his heart against her chest.

"*Danke, Gott*," she heard him whisper against her *kapp*. He pulled back, and she saw moisture in his eyes. "I never thought *Gott* would send a woman into my life capable of seeing past my scars. How did He send you?"

"He had this all in hand from the beginning, I think." Her voice sounded ragged. "How else can you explain the series of events that led to this?" Her grip around his neck tightened. "Oh, Aaron, I love you."

"November," he pronounced with the smile she had come to love. "No later than November. You'll be baptized by then, and we can be married shortly after."

"November," she agreed.

Epilogue

Miriam drove her car through the town of Pierce, one of the last times she ever hoped to drive the vehicle. She was tired but pleased after sitting for the National Nurse–Midwife Certification examination in Missoula. Now, after a long drive, she was almost home. The late-October colors were bright, but the mountaintops already had a dusting of winter's first snow.

In town, she noticed Aaron's horse and buggy hitched in front of the attorney's office. She grinned. She knew he was signing contracts today for the manufacture and production of his milking device, and she couldn't wait to hear how it went.

She passed through town and turned down the gravel road leading to the Amish settlement. Within ten minutes, she'd pulled into her brother's driveway and guided the vehicle around to the back, to her cabin.

On the porch was a large box. Miriam knew what it was but didn't want to open it until Aaron was with her.

Until he finished with his business, she continued packing. She was sorry to leave behind the darling little guesthouse her brother had built for her, but since she and Aaron would be married within two weeks, she would be moving into his cabin right after the wedding. The only sound aside from the clock ticking over the door was her happy humming as she worked.

An hour later, just as dusk was falling, she heard his knock on her door. "Come in!"

He entered, grinning, and Miriam dropped what she was doing and threw herself into his arms. "I missed you."

He kissed her, then leaned back with his arms looped around her waist. "How did the examination go?"

"It went well. I had so much experience from my work in Indiana—not to mention, I was already certified there—that I could practically answer the questions in my sleep. Do you want some tea?"

"*Ja*, please."

As she prepared it, she told him about her day. "Once I get the certification, the last step is to apply to the state's Board of Nursing to practice midwifery in Montana," she concluded. "Not that I intend to deliver babies anywhere but here in the community, but it does mean I can access hospital facilities in Pierce if there's an emergency."

Aaron sat at the tiny kitchen table with a grin. "I'm so glad to see you back to doing what you like best."

She blew him a kiss. "What I like best is knowing I'm going to be your wife soon." She handed him a mug. "Now, tell me what happened with the contracts."

He dipped the tea strainer in and out of the hot water. "I'm glad I took Benjamin's advice to have the attorney review everything," he said. "He was able to negotiate an extra percentage point. Buck Winston will become the manufacturer for the milking device. He will license the invention and pay me royalties based on the net factory sales of the milkers. The attorney was able to negotiate those royalties from five to six percent, which is actually very generous."

"That's wonderful!" Miriam felt a glow of pride for her soon-to-be-husband's clever mind.

"And I have more news." His eyes gleamed. "Buck wants me to expand the line. He suggested a solar-powered milker or a battery-powered milker. In other words, I'm going to have my work cut out for me for the foreseeable future."

Miriam didn't mention what seemed like the greatest blessing of all: Aaron had returned from town—one of many such trips he'd taken in the last couple of months—and made no mention of the strangers' reactions to his face. In his fired-up enthusiasm over the production of his invention, it was almost as if he forgot all about how he looked and instead merely concentrated on the job at hand. "*Danke*, *Gott*," she thought to herself.

When he finished telling her about the events of the day, Miriam mentioned the package she had received. "It's from my sister-in-law, Esther, in Indiana."

"Is that what I think it is?" Aaron grinned.

"*Ja*, I'm pretty sure it is. Shall we open it?"

"You bet!"

Miriam took a pair of scissors and carefully sliced open the strapping tape on the box. She peeled back the flaps. Inside was a cloth bag, and pinned to the bag's opening was a note.

"With *Gott*'s blessing for a marriage as happy as ours," it read, and was signed by both Esther and her brother Joseph.

"I can't wait to meet them both when they come visit for the wedding," Aaron remarked.

"And they'll be staying here in the cabin too. Thomas can't wait to see them."

"Open the bag!" urged Aaron.

Miriam opened the drawstring closure of the cloth bag and withdrew a quilt. She unfolded it and gasped. Even Aaron drew in his breath as the full beauty of the bed covering was revealed.

Esther was an expert quilter, and it seemed she had poured her heart and soul into this wedding gift. It was made with her sister-in-law's characteristic puzzle-pattern shapes. But in this case, the pieces were tiny and formed stunning imagery hinting at mountains and meadows and snow, almost like a real puzzle. The colors shimmered—green and gold and brown, with hints of red and blue. It was the perfect gift for a Montana wedding.

Aaron took one side and she took the other, and they spread the quilt open on the floor, then simply stood and admired it.

"I don't think I've ever seen anything so beautiful," she breathed at last.

"Maybe not, but I have." Aaron slipped an arm around her waist and looked into her eyes.

"Oh, Aaron, you say the sweetest things." She felt her eyes fill with happy tears.

"In two weeks, this will cover our marriage bed." His arm tightened around her. "You've managed to tame this wild beast into someone civilized through the power of love."

She kissed him. "It wasn't hard," she murmured. "Because I could see the handsome prince inside you, waiting to be released."

"I never thought a fairy tale could come true," he said. *"Gott ist gut."*

* * * * *

Dear Reader,

Who doesn't love a fairy tale with a happy ending? I hope you enjoyed reading about Aaron and Miriam as I tried to bring their story to life.

Some of the most powerful real-life love stories involve people overcoming great challenges. One of my best friends has a debilitating disease and is confined to a wheelchair. Her marriage of three decades is one of the happiest I know. True love is so inspiring, isn't it?

I enjoy hearing from readers, so feel free to email me at patricelewis@protonmail.com.

Blessings,
Patrice

COMING NEXT MONTH FROM
Love Inspired

AN AMISH MOTHER FOR HIS CHILD
Amish Country Matches • by Patricia Johns

After giving up on romance, Verna Kauffman thought a marriage of convenience would give her everything she's longed for—a family. But marrying reserved Adam Lantz comes with a list of rules Verna wasn't expecting. Can they overcome their differences to discover that all they really need is each other?

HER SCANDALOUS AMISH SECRET
by Jocelyn McClay

A life-changing event propels Lydia Troyer to return to her Amish community to repair her damaged reputation—with a baby in tow. And when she finds old love Jonah Lapp working on her family home, she knows winning back his trust will be hardest of all...especially once she reveals her secret.

FINDING THEIR WAY BACK
K-9 Companions • by Jenna Mindel

Twenty-eight years ago, Erica Laine and Ben Fisher were engaged to be married...until Erica broke his heart. Now, as they work together on a home that Erica needs to fulfill her new role as a traveling nurse, their past connection is rekindled. But can love take root when Erica is committed to leaving again?

FOR THE SAKE OF HER SONS
True North Springs • by Allie Pleiter

Following a tragedy, Willa Scottson doesn't hold much hope for healing while at Camp True North Springs. But swim instructor Bruce Lawrence is determined to help the grieving widow and her twin boys. This is his chance to make amends—if Willa will let him once the truth comes out...

THE GUARDIAN AGREEMENT
by Lorraine Beatty

When jilted bride Olivia Marshall is forced to work with her ex-fiancé, Ben Kincaid, it stirs up old pain. Yet she finds herself asking Ben for help when her four-year-old nephew is abandoned on her doorstep. Will their truce lead to a second chance...or will Ben's past stand in their way?

SAVING THE SINGLE DAD'S BOOKSTORE
by Nicole Lam

Inheriting his grandfather's bookstore forces Dominic Tang to return to his hometown faced with a big decision—keep it or sell. But manager Gianna Marchesi insists she can prove the business's worth. Then an accident leads to expensive damages, making Dominic choose between risking everything or following his heart...

LOOK FOR THESE AND OTHER LOVE INSPIRED BOOKS WHEREVER BOOKS ARE SOLD, INCLUDING MOST BOOKSTORES, SUPERMARKETS, DISCOUNT STORES AND DRUGSTORES.

LICNM1123